# A Consternation of Monsters

# A Consternation of Monsters

stories
by Eric Fritzius

ISBN-13: 978-0692428511 (Mister Herman's Publishing Company)

ISBN-10: 0692428518

Edition 1.7

Mister Herman's Publishing Company
**http://www.misterherman.com**

Cover design and photography by Eric Fritzius
Cover cement illustrations by T.R. Dunnam
About the Author illustration by Boyd Carr

"…to a Flame" was first published in the *Mountain Voices* anthology from West Virginia Writers, Inc.

"Nigh" was first published in the *Dark Tales of Terror* anthology from Woodland Press.

This book is dedicated to my dad,
who taught me how to tell stories,
and without whom there would be no Hocco…

to Belinda Anderson, my writing mentor,
without whom most of these stories
would have had no deadline…

to Marcus Hammack, who gave me Z…

and to Joe Evans, my ideal reader,
who also gave me the line about the fork.

# Contents


| | |
|---|---|
| **Foreword** | |
| **The Hocco Makes the Echo** | **1** |
| **Nigh** | **16** |
| **Old Country** | **21** |
| **...to a Flame** | **51** |
| **Wolves Among Stones at Dusk** | **64** |
| **The Ones That Aren't Crows** | **78** |
| **The Wise Ones** | **91** |
| **The King's Last Nacho** | **115** |
| **Puppet Legacy** | **145** |
| **Limited Edition** | **168** |
| **About the Author** | **209** |

# Foreword

## by Rik Winston, host of *UFO All Night*

Monsters are my bread and butter. My radio show, *UFO All Night* (check your local listings) largely revolves around them. And every night I take call after call from listeners who claim to have seen them—be they the little green ones who fly unidentified in our skies or the ones who leave behind only giant footprints and blurry photos. I also take calls from those few deluded souls who still insist monsters do not exist in the first place (he types with a wink and a smile). I have to think about monsters quite a lot. One of the things I've never wondered about monsters, though, is what might be a good collective noun to describe them.

Most of us know the standard collective nouns of nature: swarm of bees, gaggle of geese, pack of wolves, pride of lions, herd of cattle, pod of whales, school of fish, team of horses, and the one people like to cite the most, a murder of crows. But there are far better, more creatively-conceived, collective nature nouns out there. Dig around just a little and you'll find a mob of emus, an army of frogs, a busyness of ferrets, a sneak of weasels, an array of hedgehogs, a parliament of owls, and a cackle of hyenas, among many others.

Another I particularly enjoy is an unkindness of ravens. However, the collective noun I find most apropos to primates of all shades is: a shrewdness of apes. Monsters, though? Never once considered it.

A *consternation* is the collective description your author, Mr. Fritzius, came up with for monsters.[1] It's not easy to remember, sure, but it has a nice alliteration to it. Merriam Webster defines it as: *a strong feeling of surprise or sudden disappointment that causes confusion.* Describes the feelings generated in the typical monster encounter perfectly. Who's going to argue with him?

Naturally, the internet.

Trouble is, folks online can't seem to agree on a term of their own, either, or whether or not one should even exist. Most seem happy to argue that because the term *monster* does not describe a single species in the first place, applying a collective noun to it is a useless proposition and that no one should bother to try.[2] (I have a collective noun for a lot of those people too, but it's not a term I could use on the air so I'll avoid it in print as well.) I disagree with them.

While monsters may come in many different forms and even different species (a few of which may yet prove to be real, living, breathing, formerly-legendary animals someday), the base idea of *the*

---

[1] At least he didn't call it *a mash.*

[2] One wise soul, David Malki, the brain behind the fantastic online comic *Wondermark*, has created a list of collective nouns for various classes of supernatural creatures found in literature and legend. Among the ones he has provided that I love are: an academy of apparitions, a racket of banshees, a penumbra of spirits, a solace of Baba Yaga, a drove of elves, a fondle of unicorns, a clubbing of chupacabra, a ruminance of bigfeet, and an audacity of gargoyles. But he offers none for monsters as a whole.

*monster*—the unknown thing in the darkness—is one of the most powerful concepts in history, and one found across all cultures. Monsters, in this way, have been with us from the dawn of time, have accompanied our species on its journey across the ages, and even now lurk in the darkened corners of the allegedly enlightened world of the 21st century. The archetype monster alone deserves a collective noun.

Let me tell you a story about monsters and your author's home turf of West Virginia…

Once or twice a year, representatives from one of the various cable television channels devoted to learning, science or history phone me up to ask if I'd like to host a television version of my radio show. For various reasons—my being the antithesis of telegenic possibly one—it's never quite worked out. But, every year they try again and once in a while they throw enough money at me that I venture forth from my comfortable broadcast studio to investigate the strange and unusual out in the real world. This is how I found myself in Durbin, West Virginia, back in the mid-oughts.

West Virginia is a state with a fairly large pedigree when it comes to the strange and unusual—some of which you'll learn about in this very collection. I could probably do a whole TV series set there—and others have tried. Durbin itself is not precisely a weird place, though. It's a beautiful-yet-tiny community smack in the middle of the Monongahela National Forest, not far from the National Radio Astronomy Observatory at Green Bank. And it is a place that has remained largely unchanged for most of the past century. You can stand on the main drag through town—US 250, right across from the bright yellow train station of their scenic railroad, the Durbin Rocket—and other than the Coke machine in front of the general store, you'd swear you had been transported back to the 1940s or earlier. We were there to use the Durbin Rocket to recreate footage for a story about the Ghost of Silver Run.[3]

One of the locals who'd been watching us film approached me for an autograph, and he happened to mention that he too had once seen something strange akin to a ghost. He was hesitant to spell it out at first, but I could tell from his manner that whatever he'd seen had shaken him so badly that the very memory threatened to overcome him right then. I had to know his story. With some encouragement, he explained that, as a teenager, he had once heard some odd noises coming from atop the tin roof of his family's barn. He crept out into the night, his daddy's shotgun in hand, only to find that the noises were being made by the boot-clad heels of a figure standing atop the barn. And that figure, he told me in a whisper, was none other than a headless horseman.

That's right, a *headless horseman.*

A horseman who, for reasons we can never be completely certain of due to the passage of time, no longer possesses a head.[4]

---

[3] Lady on a train got killed, came back to haunt the Silver Run Tunnel. The real Silver Run, north in Ritchie County, lacks a proper historic train engine, such as the Durbin Rocket.

[4] Or, for that matter, a horse, since there was no mention of one accompanying the figure atop the barn. How the man knew it was a *horseman*, per se, remains unclear. Spurs maybe?

Now, I know what you're thinking: "*Headless horseman? Riiiiight. That guy was yanking your chain, Rik.*" And, logically, you'd be right. In our allegedly enlightened times, the very idea that a headless horseman actually exists, not to mention that someone would admit to seeing it, is utterly absurd. I wanted to reject it outright myself, except that I had seen the man's face as he told his story and he was one scared dude. Which isn't to say he wasn't crazy, or hadn't been sipping from a jar of Eldridge County moonshine before he saw his horseman. But he fully believed he had seen himself a monster that night long ago.

Most people would dismiss the man's tale as legend and folklore. Those labels are often slapped onto strange and unusual concepts that are not openly accepted. The trouble with dismissing legends and folklore, though, is that, like their cousins *religion* and *mythology*, there is at the heart of them a hard kernel of belief. At some point in history, someone believed in these monsters and legends powerfully enough that they passed the information on—be it in oral accounts, cave paintings, or the printed word. These legends and myths always make for fantastic stories, because deep down we'd really like to believe them. In the face of all evidence to the contrary, we *want* to believe. And belief, my friends, is a powerful thing. You can dismiss it if you like, but I don't advise it. To do so is like trying to dismiss a barrel of mercury—it's slippery, beady stuff and if you can't keep all of it in the barrel, you're in serious trouble. Oh, and it might just kill you if you're not careful with it.

I did not then, nor do I now dismiss the man's account of the headless horseman of Durbin, just as I also do not dismiss the Mothman of Point Pleasant, nor the Monster of Flatwoods, nor the Hocco of Mississippi, nor the various gods, angels, shadowy mobsters, Men in Black, wise old women, or once-and-future kings of rock & roll that also appear in this collection. Or the monsters. You'll find a whole consternation of them in these pages.[5] And it's an apt term for them, because those of us who want to believe are forever in a state of consternation over the reality of such creatures, just as we would be *consternated* were we ever to meet one ourselves.

A warning: the monsters you'll find here don't always lurk forth baring fangs and claws, either. Often, they simply walk on two legs—we shrewd apes often being the most monstrous of God's creatures.

I've not yet met the author of this book. I can tell from his work, though, he knows a thing or two about the power of belief. I bet he knows the fear of it, too. He also seems to know that the best way to get my attention and to secure my services at writing heavily-footnoted introductions is to drop my name into one of his stories. Next time I'm in the Mountain State, we'll have to have a beer. Or maybe share a sip or two from a jar of that Eldridge County mountain nectar.

— Rik Winston

---

[5] As well as members of an unkindness, a pod, a penumbra, a pack, a sneak, and possibly a solace to boot.

# The Hocco Makes the Echo

Rob Hughes thought his kid was a genius—or, if not a genius, at least a very smart boy. Aaron was only five years old and already he could tie his shoes, count to 120, identify pictures of animals in books and recognize the constellation of Orion. Sure, he referred to it as '*Oh-wyan*,' but he knew it when he saw it; Rob had taught him that. One of Rob's friends, C.C. Mills, had a teenage son named Davis who had been studying constellations since receiving a telescope two Christmases ago. Davis had been showing off his knowledge in the Mills' front yard one night, pointing out such common sights as the big and little dippers, the Pleiades and Andromeda. Rob had then pointed into the sky and asked Aaron to identify a different constellation, to which then four-year-old Aaron piped up, "*Oh-wyan!*" That surprised the hell out of everyone. Everyone, that is, except Rob Hughes. To Rob it was merely proof of what he'd been saying all along. His boy was a genius, who had kissed the Blarney Stone somewhere around birth and could talk the ear off of anyone who stood still long enough. People could not believe he was only in Kindergarten.

"Don't go too far out there now," Aaron's papaw said from the porch swing. It was dusk and Rob and Aaron were standing in the yard in front of his in-laws' backwoods Wayne County, Mississippi farm. The property was surrounded by an expanse of pine trees broken only by a red dirt road that ran in front of the farm, along Papaw's 180 acres of property. The rain from earlier in the day had pooled in a low cypress patch next to the pines and a mist rose from it, hugging the ground as it spread into the forest itself.

"I said, don't go too far out there," Papaw repeated. "It gets boggy."

"We heard you, Papaw," Aaron sang.

"Hope so. You track mud on your Mamaw's carpet she'll wear you both out."

"Your papaw's got the right idea," Rob said. "Better get you off the ground so you don't get us worn out."

Aaron giggled, then held out his arms like Superman as he was lifted off the grass and seated across the back of Rob's shoulders. They walked out into the yard, past the rope swing that hung from a branch of the big oak by the driveway and stopped by the row of plants and bushes that grew at the edge of the regularly mowed section of the yard. There they were met by an oddity of Papaw's farm: the creepy tree.

There were, truth be told, a number of other oddities to be found on Papaw's farm. The old smoke house, for instance, which Papaw himself had constructed from homemade cement blocks when Rob's late wife, Jean, was a child. These days it was used more as a workshop and a place to store Papaw's snuff than it was for smoking meat. What made the little building odd, though, were the designs set into the cement blocks themselves. Most of them were innocent enough, like the leaf impressions and handprints made by Jean and her sister Della. Others, like the etched faces set into the corner stones, were vaguely disturbing. The modestly drawn faces bore extreme emotions, such as "surprise," "anger," or "fright terror," and were labeled as such in the cement itself. Rob found it strange that there were no more positive emotions represented among the faces. He seemed to remember Jean once telling him that they had been copied from an old book, but Rob wasn't sure of the details.

The creepy tree was another matter. Rob supposed that the creepy tree was not so much a tree as it was a tree branch—gnarled and old and dead for a very long time. It was secured to the stump of a buried fence post via a thick well-rusted metal bolt. The creepy tree forked mid-way up its height. One of its limbs curved toward the ground, but did not quite touch it. The other limb curled up and then around upon itself in a most unnatural manner, as though it had been broken over at some point during its life then continued to grow in the new direction. The end of this deformed limb intersected with a third limb, perhaps from a separate tree which had made the mistake of growing too close to the first. The third limb had been sawed from its original tree, leaving it entwined with the main limb of the creepy tree, forming a knot of wood. A rose bush had been planted next to the post stump and its thorny vines had grown around the unnatural host structure like gray barbed wire, enhancing the vague air of menace surrounding it.

Rob had always supposed that Papaw had found the two trees grown together and cut away the odd limbs and bolted it to the post to form the creepy tree. The other possibility was that he had somehow engineered it as some kind of organic sculpture. It would have taken years or possibly decades to accomplish, but Rob didn't put it past the old man. There was scarcely a tree on the property that hadn't had a branch from another tree grafted onto it at some point. On papaw's farm, there were apple trees that bore pears and peach trees that bore plums. This and the fact that there was a remarkably similar creepy tree bolted in the front yard of Papaw's nearest neighbor, "Old Man" Manning, led Rob to believe this might not have been an accident. Rob had once asked Papaw about the two trees and the reason they existed. He didn't recall receiving a satisfactory answer, but had finally chalked it up to some kind of backwoods superstition.

"I hear crickets," Aaron said.

"Oh, yeah. Plenty of them," Rob said, pausing to listen to the crickets, birds and other assorted nocturnal creatures, warming up for the night's performance. "Can you hear that deeper chirping?" Rob asked. "Sounds like *wok wok wok.*"

"Yeah."

"You know what makes that sound?"

Aaron seemed to think about it for a moment. "Big crickets?"

Rob laughed. "No. Those are frogs."

"Nuh uh. Frogs say *ribbit*!"

"Yeah, but the little ones sound like they're chirping," Rob said. They listened for several seconds. "Now listen to this," Rob said. He held his hands up on either side of his mouth and shouted "Hello!" In the distance, they heard the shout echo *"hello."* Rob cocked his head to the side and was not surprised to see a quizzical expression on Aaron's face above.

"Hello!" Rob shouted again.

*"hello"* the echo answered again.

Now an array of expressions crossed Aaron's face, from elation to confusion. This was something altogether new for the boy and he didn't seem sure what to make of it. Rob decided to let him in on the secret. "That's an echo. The sound of my voice is bouncing off the trees."

Aaron's lips mashed together and he looked suspiciously at the forest for several seconds. "Hocco," he said.

"No, Aaron. It's called an echo."

"Hocco."

"No, son. Say it with me. Eh-ko. Echo."

"The Hocco *makes* the echo, Daddy."

"No. Nothing makes the echo. Well, nothing out there. We make the sound, but it bounces off the trees and comes back to our ears as an echo. See? Here, listen. Hamburglar!" Rob shouted. From the forest the word *"hamburglar"* echoed back. Rob shouted again. "Mister Snuffleupagus."

*"...fellupagus,"* the echo said.

"Well, if you do one that's too long it covers itself up," Rob said. "See, it's only an echo. Just like I told you."

Aaron was quiet for a moment, then said, "The Hocco makes the echo."

Rob grunted and his teeth clinched slightly. It was irritating that his genius son didn't seem to be grasping this relatively simple concept. They'd had the same sort of trouble during a car trip the previous summer when Aaron insisted that the white sand on the banks of a distant creek bed was actually snow. It had angered Rob that his son wouldn't accept his word that it was not snow, until Rob realized that Aaron was only pretending in the first place. The kid knew that it was really sand, no matter how much he might have wished it had been snow. He just loved to make-believe. Aaron was always making up imaginary friends or giving names and personalities to his stuffed animals and other inanimate objects. No deficiencies in the imagination department for Rob Hughes's boy, that was for sure.

"A *hocko*, you say?" Rob asked, deciding to play along for the moment. "Where is the hocko?"

Aaron pointed toward the woods.

"I don't see it. What does it look like?" Rob asked. Aaron didn't answer, though. Rob looked up at him and saw the boy's expression shift with a purity that made Rob's scalp tingle. Somewhere in that boy's head, gears were meshing. He decided to try another angle.

"Why does the hocko make echoes?"

Again Aaron was silent for a moment.

"The Hocco's trying to find you. It says everything you say so you'll keep saying stuff. Then it follows the sound. And then it *gets* you."

"What happens when the hocko *gets* you?" Rob asked. Aaron didn't answer. "Come on. You can tell me. What happens?"

Aaron closed his mouth tight and shook his head rapidly from side to side.

"You know what I think?" Rob said, slowly sneaking his hands along the sides of Aaron's legs. "I think the hocko creeps through the woods real slow 'til he finds a little boy and then… and then… he tickles him!" Rob grabbed Aaron's stomach, tickling him furiously causing a burst of giggles and squeals. The tickling lasted for nearly half a minute, ending only when Rob began to lose his balance and took a step forward for support. Aaron's squeals immediately turned to a scream which echoed back from the trees, slightly muted. Aaron heard the echo and clapped a hand over his mouth. It would almost have been comical had there not been fear and tears in the boy's eyes.

"Hey, kiddo. What's the matter? Why are you crying?"

"I want to go in the house, Daddy," Aaron sobbed.

"Why? I thought you were having fun?"

Aaron shook his head.

"You're not scared of the echoes, are you? Because you don't need to be. It's just sound bouncing off the trees. Listen… Echo!" Rob shouted.

"*...echo,*" came the reply from the trees.

Aaron shook his head again. "The Hocco makes the…"

"No, Aaron. It doesn't. The hocko doesn't make any echoes because there isn't any hocko. He's make-believe. Just like on Mr. Rogers." Rob then wished he hadn't mentioned Mr. Rogers at all. *Mr. Rogers' Neighborhood* was not one of Rob's favorite shows. He didn't see the sense in Fred Rogers telling kids that the *Neighborhood of Make-Believe* wasn't real then disproving this by showing them physical sets and puppet characters that really existed. He also thought Mr. Rogers was too much of a sissy to be a good influence for Aaron. Rob made a mental note to add Mr. Rogers to the list of shows his son was forbidden to watch.

"I want to go inside," Aaron said.

"Not yet. Not until you learn that echoes are nothing to be afraid of." Rob stepped past the creepy tree and began walking down the slope of the yard toward the cypresses and the woods beyond. "Echo!" he shouted, but he only heard part of the reply because Aaron began to fidget around his neck.

"No, Daddy. I want to go inside, now," Aaron said in a hushed whisper.

Rob was tired of this hocko foolishness. There was a place for pretending, sure, but letting his son be overcome with fear of a make-believe creature was not something he was going to stand by and allow. He knew other parents that would have dropped the subject in the name of child appeasement, but he wasn't one of them.

"Just listen," Rob said. He began walking toward the trees, defiantly shouting, "There's no such thing as hockos!"

*"...uch thing as hoccos,"* came the echo.

"No, Daddy, no..." Aaron sobbed, squirming on Rob's shoulders. It seemed as though he was trying to climb on top of Rob's head to get further from the ground. The boy was pulling his legs up and holding a tight grip on Rob's forehead with his arms.

"Stop that," Rob said. He was so distracted that he didn't see that the ground was becoming boggy until it was too late. His foot squished down into a wet patch of grass, but didn't stick. Aaron continued to wiggle and climb, trying to get his feet under him atop Rob's shoulders. In the process, Aaron's knee came up hard beneath his father's left ear, bending its lobe up, slightly tearing the connective skin between it and his neck. Rob screamed, bringing one hand to his injured ear and the other flailing to grab Aaron's arm to keep him from falling off. He caught the arm awkwardly, just as Aaron was slipping off his shoulders, and managed to pull him back up into a semi-seated position before using both hands to lower the boy to the ground.

"What do you think you're doing?" Rob yelled. "You don't hurt daddy like that!"

Instead of sobbing uncontrollably as Rob expected, though, Aaron wasn't listening at all. His eyes were staring wide at the woods. Rob turned to see what he was looking at and his body flinched. He thought he saw a shape… something, moving swiftly behind the trees. Then it was gone. Only then did it occur to Rob that he had heard no echo after his scream a few seconds ago. A chill crept up Rob's back. The crickets, frogs and birds had become profoundly silent. In fact, the only sound Rob could hear at all was the blood rushing behind his ears as his eyes strained against the failing light for any further movement in the trees.

"Time to come in," a voice from behind him said. Rob nearly jumped out of his skin, spinning around to come face to face with Papaw. The old man held an expression that meant business. "Mamaw's got Aaron's bath ready," he said.

Rob cast one last glance at the trees but saw nothing there. Aaron was still staring at them, though his eyes didn't hold quite as much fear as before. "Come on, Aaron," Rob said, touching the boy's shoulder. "Let's go in."

Inside, Aaron submitted to his bath without the usual struggle and seemed, after an hour or so, to return to his normal self. Rob continued to ponder what had occurred earlier, trying to make sense of it. He decided that the reason he hadn't heard his own echo was because he had been too distracted by the injury to his ear. In fact, come to think of it, the injury itself might have impaired his hearing for a few seconds. And he hadn't actually seen anything moving in the trees. It had been dim out, making it much easier to think you were seeing things when you really weren't. Even if he had seen something, it was probably a deer—the woods were full of them here. It was all perfectly explainable.

When Mamaw announced, at 9 p.m., that it was time for all boys to be in bed, Aaron didn't raise a protest, but asked his father if he would come to bed, too. They retired to the back bedroom of Papaw's little brick farmhouse and climbed into the double bed with the brown, painted metal frame. As usual, Rob was about to read Aaron his nightly bedtime story, but thought better of it. The only book they had brought for their visit was the *Gateway to Mystery* illustrated collection of short mystery stories. Aaron liked it because it had a painted picture of Sherlock Holmes on the cover, though there was only one Arthur Conan Doyle story in the book. The rest were written by such greats as Charles Dickens, Edgar Allan Poe, Robert Louis Stevenson and Anton Chekhov. Rob almost wished he'd never bought it in the first place. The stories all seemed to have an air of menace to them that didn't seem appropriate for Aaron's age, especially now considering the excitement earlier in the evening. In the interest of preventing nightmares Rob decided to forego the bedtime story. He was, however, careful to turn on the night-light near the bed—merely for Aaron's benefit.

Sleep itself came fitfully. Outside, the crickets and frogs were especially loud, even through the glass of the windows. Whippoorwills sang *Chipped the widow's white-oak,* beckoning to one another in some birdy mating ritual. And in the distance, hound dogs bayed to their masters after treeing some unfortunate critter. Rob lay there, listening to these sounds, not sleeping and cursing quietly to himself that the animals of the world were conspiring against his slumber. As if that weren't enough, he also had to pee. Since there would definitely be no sleep without first divesting himself of the half pitcher of iced tea with which he had washed down his supper, Rob got up and walked through the darkened house to go to the toilet.

The bathroom was located in the center of the house, just off of the dining room, but to get there Rob had to walk from the back bedroom, through the empty middle bedroom then through the living room and dining room, with only the light from the windows to guide him. Still, Rob managed to make it all the way to the bathroom without stubbing a toe in the darkness. After first shutting the adjoining door that led into Papaw and Mamaw's bedroom, Rob peed, wondering for the umpteenth time why anyone would put the one and only toilet right next to the dining room. He had asked Papaw about that one time and had been informed that he was welcome to go use the old outhouse in the chicken coop out back, which had been the primary toilet before they turned a spare closet into a bathroom back in the mid-'50s.

Rob's toes were not as lucky on the return trip through the living room. In the darkness, he stubbed his right big toe on the edge of the wood-burning heater in the living room. He immediately launched into a fit of cursing that was almost completely drowned out by the resonating clang from the heater's metal housing. Another sound was almost drowned out as well, though not one originating from the heater. Rob barely noticed it at first, but caught the tail end of it as the clang and his cursing died down. Outside, in the distance, there was a shout. He paused to listen and heard it again.

"*...hello.*"

Rob shook his head violently from side to side, trying to shake off the drowsiness that was obviously welling up in him. He didn't want to admit it, didn't want to even think it, but the distant shout he heard sounded exactly like his own voice. At this point, he wanted to be wide awake in the hope that what he had heard had been in his own imagination. It hadn't been a bird or crickets making the noise, for they were again silent.

"*...hamburglar,*" came another shout from outside. It sounded closer this time. Rob didn't know what was happening, but that chilly feeling had returned to his spine.

As he reached the middle bedroom, he saw the door of the back room illuminated by the night-light. He was half-way to that door when the light began to flicker. He didn't remember it flickering before, but it was certainly providing intermittent light now. It continued to flicker on and off until Rob reached the back room, at which point the light winked out entirely.

*"Mister Snuffleupagus!"* his own voice shouted outside, now from the front yard. Then there was another sound. It was very similar to the sound of a weed being torn out of the ground by its roots, only

much louder. It was accompanied by the sound of splintering wood. Then something solid crashed into the front of the house, shattering one of the windows behind Rob, in the living room. Whatever object had been thrown fell away from the window, clattering to the cement porch surface.

"Aaron, wake up," Rob said moving toward the bed in the darkness. He had to get his son out of there. He didn't know where they would go, but anywhere else seemed wise at the moment. Papaw had plenty of guns. Maybe they could get one and hole up in a closet. And where was Papaw anyway? The man could hear possums in the garden at midnight, but wasn't up after all the noise outside?

*"Echo!"* came a shout from the front porch.

Rob felt the covers of the bed, touching the place where Aaron had slept, but his son wasn't there. He turned on the bedside lamp, but its filament popped instantly. The afterimage of the flash afforded Rob a view of the bed that told him that Aaron was indeed missing from it.

"Aaron! Aaron, where are you?" he whispered.

The night-light flickered to life again, sending shadows dancing. Rob turned and for only a second saw the shadow of something dark and cat-like reflected on the wall. It had tall ears. Then the light went out and remained out.

*"There's no such thing as Hoccos!"* the Hocco echoed.

Within the closet of the back bedroom, buried beneath three layers of spare blankets, Aaron cried and tried with all his might to block out the sounds he could hear just outside the closet door.

He had always been a very smart boy.

# Nigh

Helen St. John, *Starbucks* employee #73451, looked on as her de facto training-supervisor, Ted (#42752), expertly mixed a house blend double latte, slipped a cardboard-cozy onto the cup and slid it across the counter to a man holding a yellow picket sign.

"Still look like tomorrow?" Ted asked, while ringing up the order.

The man with the sign absently looked up at the boy and said, "Yes. Definitely tomorrow."

Helen thought the man was in his late fifties, though it was difficult to tell through the thick salt-and-pepper beard and long stringy dark hair. His clothing was quite ragged, but he didn't smell too bad.

"I'll keep a cup warm for you just in case it doesn't," Ted said with a wry smile.

The man with the sign nodded, accepted his change from Ted, then took his coffee and began moving toward the front door.

"You getting the hang of all this, so far?" Ted asked Helen.

"I think so. It's not too hard," she said. "Who was that guy, anyway?"

"That's Mr. Daniels—one of our regulars. He's been in for his double latte every morning since we opened three years ago. And I heard he came in the old diner that used to be here for years before that. Every single day. He's kind of a local fixture, I guess."

"Does he always carry that sign?"

"Oh, '*The End is Nigh!*' Spooky, huh? He thinks the world's going to end tomorrow."

"The way things are going these days, who could argue with him?"

Ted laughed. "Well, the thing is, Mr. Daniels thinks the world will end tomorrow *every day.*"

"Every day?"

"Yep."

"He comes in every day and says the world will end tomorrow?"

"That's about the size of it."

"Well, that's original, I guess. And here I thought he was just some crazy homeless guy."

"No. I think he has a home. This is just what he does."

"Walking up and down the sidewalk, predicting the world will end tomorrow?" Helen asked.

"Pretty much. They say he used to teach religion at some Ivy League school up north, but got fired. He supposedly taught here at

WVU for a while, but gave it up to pace the sidewalks full time. And that was like, twenty years ago, or something."

Helen shook her head. "Well, I don't know what theology he's into, but he needs to reread his Bible. Remember back at the Millennium when all the TV preachers were predicting the end? I used to worry a lot about that kind of thing. Well my daddy's a Baptist minister and he told me to just remember *Mark 13:32... 'No one knows about that day or hour, not even the angels in heaven, nor the Son, but only the Father.'* That verse made me feel a lot better. And it's true. Mr. Daniels can predict all he wants, but only God knows when the end's truly going to come. It's not coming a day sooner or later than *He* wants it to."

"Uh, yeah. Whatever," Ted said, a little suspiciously. "Um, did I show you how to work the milk jet yet?"

From outside, there came a sudden screech of tires followed by a thunk. Helen looked up in time to see a paper cup strike the front window, spraying milky brown coffee across it.

"Somebody call 911!!" a lady near the window shouted and Ted immediately snatched up the nearest phone and began dialing. Helen, however, found herself moving toward the front of the store. Beyond the brown wash on the window, she could see a shiny black luxury car—an Infiniti, she thought—parked half-way on the sidewalk. The front of its hood was dented. Helen reached the front door and knew what she would find when she opened it.

Lying in front of the car was Mr. Daniels. He was bleeding heavily from the side of his head and some of his blood had spattered onto the yellow picket sign. He looked up with tear-filled eyes as Helen knelt down beside him. His breathing was labored, but he was still trying to speak. Helen had to lean close to hear his whispers.

"Tomorrow," he said. "Maybe the day after…" With that said, his breathing stopped.

"Help! Does anyone know CPR?" Helen screamed at the bystanders around them. No one responded, but she continued to scream until she heard the sound of the *Infiniti's* driver-side door opening. Climbing out of the vehicle was a young man with long, pale blond hair. He was very tall and wore a suit made of snow-white cloth. He was the most beautiful creature she had ever seen. When his gaze fell upon her, though, Helen felt as though she was suddenly at the bottom of a cold, dark lake. She was terrified and exalted, but somehow found her voice.

"Why?" she asked, uncertain as to what exactly she meant by it. For what seemed a long time, the young man simply stared at her with those piercing eyes, the color and depth of starlight.

"Just business," the driver said.

An ambulance soon arrived to collect Mr. Daniels' body, but no one else seemed to notice that the tall young man and his Infiniti were gone, nor that they had been there at all. Witnesses described the hit-and-run culprit to police as a balding, middle-aged man in a plaid sport coat, driving a beige Buick Skylark. They all agreed on the sport coat. Only Helen knew otherwise, but no one thought to ask her. In fact, no one—not even Ted—seemed aware that she had not returned to work. Helen remained on the sidewalk, cradling the stained yellow picket sign in her lap.

*"The End is Nigh,"* it read.

Helen St. John had the strangest feeling she would soon be needing it. If not tomorrow, then perhaps the day after.

# Old Country

Martin Riscili hung up the telephone and sat down at his kitchen table. It seemed a natural thing to do, considering he had just experienced the most disturbing and surreal phone call of his life. It beat out by several degrees the time two of Martin's ex-girlfriends had phoned within five minutes of one another to tell him they might be pregnant. He'd dodged two bullets that time, for they were both merely late. Now it appeared as if he would have to dodge another—perhaps literally.

Four minutes previous, Martin had picked up the receiver of his telephone to hear the voice of Jimmy Jambalaya.

"Marty? It's Jimmy. Glad you're home." The fact that Jimmy Jambalaya was phoning at all was nothing to be happy about. Jimmy Jambalaya had never phoned before, but the list of things he might want to discuss, even considering the events of the past week, would be a short one.

"Marty, I just wanted to call and extend my condolences on the loss of your pops."

"Oh," Martin said, surprised. "Well. Thank you."

"Please. I should have told you at the funeral. Your pops was a great man. He didn't deserve to go out like that. In fact, I gave up the smokes myself as soon as I heard what he had."

Martin wasn't aware that leukemia could be caused by smoking, but there was no good reason to mention this to Jimmy Jambalaya. "Good. Good for you," he said.

"Your pops, he—" There was a pause and for a second Martin thought that Jimmy Jambalaya, cold-blooded killer that he was, might be getting emotional. Then that thick ham-fist of a voice returned with no trace of tears. "Your pops was one of the best earners the family's ever had. He ran things like a real pro and always kicked what he owed upstairs. I had a lot of respect for him and I was proud to work alongside him on the few occasions it was necessary."

"Mm. I'm sure he would say the same of you, Jimmy." This was a lie. Martin's father had held well-defined opinions of Jimmy Jambalaya, none of them positive.

"That's very kind of you."

"And the flowers you sent," Martin said. "We really appreciated them. My sister made it a point to mention how lovely they were." This too was a lie. Rachel had not mentioned them, but her facial expression when she had seen the clown-colored wreath, and the way her eyebrow had cocked when she read the name on the card, had made clear her opinion of both flowers and sender.

"It's the least I could do," Jimmy Jambalaya said.

There followed a long and uncomfortable silence. Martin tried to think of something else to say, some nugget of small talk that would lead them closer to the end of the conversation. Words failed him. Jimmy Jambalaya wasn't helping, either. It was like he was waiting for Martin to say something else—something specific.

"Listen, Marty," Jimmy Jambalaya said after several more awkward seconds passed. "I know it's a rough time for you, but we got some business between us needs taken care of."

"Yeah?"

"I hate to bring it up—you still being in grief, and all—but we're going to need your help."

Help? Jimmy Jambalaya needed his help? This was an unexpected and unwelcome turn of events.

"Sure. Fine," Martin said, trying to keep a positive tone. "Anything to help."

"Glad to hear it," Jimmy Jambalaya said. "See, me and the boys were down at the Can Can a few days ago and we were talking about a few of the, uh, weaker members of our organization. The unpleasant subject of retirements was raised and we all agreed that there might need to be a few, if you get my meaning."

"I'm… I'm not sure I do, Jimmy. I mean, I think I do, but I've never been involved in any… retirements. I'm not really in the life, you know?"

"We know, Marty. We know you're not in the life. It's how your pop always wanted it and we respect that. But this time, we're going to need your help."

Martin didn't know how to react to this. He had no illusions about what his father had done for a living and had continued to do even after the leukemia was diagnosed. Martin had always stayed out of it, though. Well, *mostly*. It had been difficult to avoid some of the more personal entanglements available to those in the life, many of which could be found at the Can Can Club.

"See, Marty, one of our *early retirees* lives out near you and we were planning on coming around to see him this afternoon."

"Uh, Jimmy, I, uh… I still don't understand how I fit into this. Do you need to use my house, or something?"

"Oh, no. Nothing like that," Jimmy Jambalaya said. "We were actually hoping to stop by and retire *you* while we were in the neighborhood and we wanted to make sure you'd be in. It's kind of a kill two birds with one stone thing—if you take my meaning."

The words had not yet sunk into Martin Riscili's head when Jimmy Jambalaya added, "Would three o'clock be good for you?" Then the phone went dead.

This was bad. This was very, very bad. This was not the sort of thing you wanted to hear on a Monday morning.

As far as Martin knew, it was unprecedented to be phoned in advance of your own hit. Most guys in the life never saw the end coming at all. They usually went out to dinner only to be gunned down on the sidewalk afterward. Or they went for one final ride after finding a friend's gun pressed to their temple. Jimmy Jambalaya's call was therefore merely an appetizer for the dinner of pain he would soon deliver. And though it was only noon now, Jimmy would not have phoned unless he was already on his way. For all Martin knew, Jimmy was calling from the driveway itself, using that new car phone he loved so much. Even if he wasn't, at the very least Martin's house was being watched by Jimmy's people. Running was not a likely option. Calling the police would also be worthless. Martin knew of several officers who were on the payroll of Jimmy Jambalaya and there were probably as many he didn't know about.

The only other person he might call was Jimmy's boss, Carlo. Martin's pop had loved Carlo like a brother, though the two of them were actually cousins, and they had always been close. There was no way Carlo would stand by and let this happen.

Sitting at his kitchen table, Martin Riscili wondered if there was something he could have said earlier in the call—perhaps during one of the awkward silences—that might have forestalled this turn of events. Phrases of apology kept knocking around in his head, such as: *"Gee, Jimmy, I'm sorry you hate my guts because I slept with your girlfriend once or twice, and may have almost knocked her up. I'm also sorry that news of the relationship got spread around and that she dumped you in front of everyone that night at the Can Can Club. If it's any consolation, she's no longer living with me. Friends?"*

Martin stood up and reached for the handset of the old hard-wired Bell rotary phone that had come with the house. There was no dial tone. He tapped the cradle to disconnect, then tapped it twice more. Still nothing. It was dead. *Damn Jimmy and his union connections!*

If staying alive was to remain on Martin's agenda, his next move was going to have to be a pretty damned wise one. The only other thing that came to mind, though, were the words of advice his grandmothers had given him thirteen years ago.

*"Keep it close to you, for you will require it. When the day of your greatest need arrives, you must take it in your hands and voice the call of old. Only then will the name of our families be restored."*

This didn't make Martin feel any better. The idea itself was, to put it lightly, crazy. At the moment, though, it seemed like his one and only hope. If only he could remember where he had put his grandmothers' quilt.

Both of Martin Riscili's grandmothers had been brought over from the old country when he was a toddler. Martin's father, Paolo—later Paul—had been in the United States for a few short years then, but had proven himself enough of an asset to the extended "family" that he could afford such luxuries as transporting dear relatives across an ocean. Refusing to fly in an airplane, the women arrived together by boat in 1952, neither speaking a word of English, nor willing to learn, nor willing to speak to one another in any language.

No one seemed to know the nature of the feud that had erupted between Grandma Riscili and Mama Cotroni. Neither would suffer the presence of the other except during large family gatherings, which became increasingly rare as the years passed. That the two women had been brought to live under the same roof with Martin and his parents did little to help matters. According to Martin's late mother, after three months of near constant fighting between the two women, Paul came up with a lasting solution. He moved them both to separate, yet equally nice hotel suites at the Alighieri, downtown. Then he called in favors from some contractors who owed him money. Within a month, he had separate but equal additions built on opposite sides of the family home, each containing its own living quarters and kitchen.

Some of Martin's best childhood memories were formed in those two kitchens. Free from the presence of the other, Martin's grandmothers softened and revealed themselves as kindly old ladies. He and his little sister were always welcome there and always well fed in their grandmother's rooms.

For a while the war between the two women seemed to grow cold, but even cold war was still war. The ultimate weapon in this war became food, which was used to lure their grandchildren away from the enemy. This was where Martin first learned to cook, a skill that would eventually bring him a good livelihood. Beyond the food, though, there were the stories. Both grandmothers were gifted storytellers and would sit—a rocking chair for Grandma Riscili, a Barca lounger for Mama Cotroni—and sew while they spun their tales. Even having grown up around family fluent in Italian, Martin only understood around every fourth word of his grandmothers' stories at first. They both tended to lapse into an older dialect that even Martin's father had difficulty understanding. As the years, cannolis, cakes, and pies passed by, though, his comprehension of their speech grew and he came to understand their tales with clarity.

The women both told long lost stories of the old country. They were rarely nice or happy stories—more like fairy tales, but with small clans of Sicilian farmers cast as heroes who defended their land from invading enemy armies, or, sometimes, their own government. The grandmothers would often illustrate their stories, too, using flat cloth dolls to represent the major characters. These they would pin to a corkboard, acting out the scenes with voices and even song.

Mama Cotroni told tales of Sparrow Salvatore, supposedly an early ancestor of Martin's who led an agrarian revolt against French invaders, winning several battles against them and proving himself leader of his clan. Her illustration of Sparrow cut a dashing figure, even in scraps of terrycloth and denim.

Grandma Riscili also told tales of Sparrow Salvatore, but in her tales he was always cast as a much more flawed figure, rendered in black and gray felt as an ugly hunched man. The hero of Grandma Riscili's tales was a wise and beautiful woman from the village named Natale. It had been Natale's idea to assemble the army of local farmers to cooperate against their common enemies—enemies which continued to come no matter how many times they were beaten back. Hers was an idea Grandma Riscili said would go on to serve their clan and neighboring clans well for centuries to come. It also served as the eventual foundation for the organization to which Martin's father had belonged. However, according to Grandma Riscili, the treacherous Sparrow Salvatore stole the credit for this successful plan, allowing him to win leadership of the clan. It was not until the French returned with reinforcements that easily overran Sparrow's army, that he once again sought the aid of the wise Natale. She proposed an alliance of a different sort.

Martin knew that alliances were important. Even at that young age, Martin knew a little about his father's career. It wasn't as glamorous as that of the pinstriped gangsters of the '30s, as portrayed in Martin's favorite old movies, or even the *Godfather* films of more recent years. But, then, his father Paul hadn't exactly been Marlon Brando, either. As Martin understood it, his father's alliances were often territorial agreements, marking out the boundaries within which business could be conducted and determining who would receive a portion of the proceeds of that business. It wasn't until much later that Martin understood what this "business" entailed, but as a boy he accepted that *business* was what his father did.

The alliances his grandmothers spoke of, however, were of a much different nature. Natale had used an ancient spell to call upon dark and fearsome warriors who came to the aid of Sparrow's army. They rode in on gigantic, black cat-beasts, laying waste to the invaders. These were always Martin's favorite stories, which he begged his grandmothers to tell and retell.

Martin heard the front door swing open. Here he had killers on the way and a potentially impossible search before him and he hadn't thought to lock the door. He grabbed the nearest weapon he could find—a butcher's knife from a slotted wooden stand on the kitchen counter. He then crept across the gray tile floor and stood behind the swinging kitchen door, hoping to remain out of sight until someone—perhaps Jimmy himself—had entered the room. Martin had never killed anyone, but decided that if he was going to start it might as well be with someone as deserving as Jimmy Jambalaya. He would try to say some Hail Marys as Jimmy's men gunned him down and hope God wouldn't look too harshly on his soul. If he was lucky, removing a monster like Jimmy Jambalaya from the Lord's creation would provide Martin some celestial credit.

"Marty?" It was Melissa's voice calling from the foyer. Martin breathed a long sigh and came out from behind the door. He did not, however, lay down his butcher's knife until he had peeked around the edge of the door frame, toward the foyer, to make certain Melissa was alone. She was standing by the still open front door wearing jeans and a sweatshirt with the sleeves cut off. This had been her standard casual look since *Flashdance* came out a few months back.

"Hey," Melissa said. "Do you know there are two guys sitting in a car out front?"

Martin's head began to swim. He still had the presence of mind to say, "Close the door."

She didn't move. "Marty? Is something wrong?"

He moved swiftly to the front door, still holding the knife at his side, and closed and locked it, then hooked the security chain. Only then did he risk peering through the peep hole. There was indeed a long brown Lincoln parked down by the street, the silhouettes of two men within it. The car belonged to Tino Bortsal, one of Jimmy's crew.

"Hell," Martin said.

"Marty, talk to me. Are you okay?"

"No," he said. Martin stared at her, a memory flashing through his mind of the first time he'd laid eyes on her, at the specialty supermarket on Clifton Street. He had been looking for mushrooms worthy of Grandma Riscili's Pappardelle con Porcini. She had been beautiful, to be sure, with that cascading blond hair, but she wasn't his usual type. Until then he had specialized in strippers who'd barely made it out of high school and more drama in their lives than was healthy—at least, healthy for him. He couldn't help that they practically flung themselves at him whenever he visited the Can Can Club—they knew who his father was, so they weren't *that* dumb. Thankfully, Melissa didn't work that way.

"You've got to get out of here. Right now."

"What are you talking about? What's going on?"

"Just go!" he said, unlocking the door again, pulling at her arm to try and get her close enough to shove her through it. He had to get her out of there. If she stayed, Jimmy would kill her just to make Martin watch.

"Marty, stop it! What are you doing?"

"Go! Those guys outside are—" Martin stopped. He was going about this the wrong way. This was Melissa. Pleading to issues of her safety wouldn't work. This required finesse.

"Mel," he said, turning to face her. "You *know* what my pop did for a living. We've been through all that. Those guys out there are friends of his and they're going to want to talk to me for a while about… his business. About money."

"What *about* money?"

"It's kind of like a… a… a pension plan, see. But they won't like it if anyone else is here. So you've got to go," he said, putting her keys into her hand.

"A pension plan? From the mob?"

"Sure. They always take care of their own and that includes family. If Ma were still alive, it would go to her, but it's just me and Rachel now. I'm going to turn it down, of course."

Melissa's eyes grew fiery. "I thought we said no secrets, Martin."

"What?"

"You're telling me you screamed at me and nearly shoved me through that door for a pension program?"

"There's no secret. It's business."

"Then why can't I be here?"

His mind raced, trying to find a way to explain why guys who wanted to discuss the finer points of avoiding inheritance tax would be lurking out front in a Lincoln Continental. He had nothing.

Melissa fixed him with a stern gaze. "It's a good thing you're *not* in the mob, Marty. You're a worthless liar."

Martin started to protest, then didn't. He looked into her eyes—those dark green eyes that were even now welling with tears—and saw she already understood why the men were here. She turned away, wiping her face with the back of her hand. He knew she wouldn't let herself come apart and it didn't surprise him in the slightest. If he had learned anything about her, it was that she could be a rock when needed and would save the emotion for later—assuming they survived.

Martin locked the front door again. He told her about Jimmy Jambalaya's call and impending arrival, though he remained sketchy as to the details of Jimmy's grudge.

"That's why you have to go," he finished.

"Not without you."

"He'll kill you."

"Then come with me."

"I can't. Tino's out there to make sure I don't go anywhere. But he can't chase you and guard me at the same time. You can get back in your car and go."

"Then we'll go to the garage. I'll drive your car out. We can put you in the trunk and they won't even see…"

*Yeah, and I'll never leave that trunk again and you'll wind up in it with me,* he thought.

"No, baby. It won't work. It has to be you. Alone."

"Then we'll call the police," she said, running for the phone in the kitchen. He heard her pick it up and dial 0. The rotary wheel spun around, clicking into place.

"It's dead."

"Yeah."

Melissa dropped the receiver. It smacked off the kitchen's tile floor and continued to spring on its cord, clattering against the wall.

"What do we do then?"

"I know this is going to sound insane," he said, "but we have to find my grandmothers' quilt."

A minute later, Martin was flinging sheets and pillowcases from his linen closet into a silk and cotton pile in the middle of the hall.

"Help me understand this, Marty," Melissa said. "Are you looking for a quilt or a chest?"

"A quilt *in* a chest. They put it in a chest."

"Your grandmothers?"

"Yes."

"How exactly is a quilt going to help you against hit men?"

“I told you it sounds insane,” Martin said, tossing another fistful of sheets aside. He considered telling her the quilt was stuffed with payoff money, but knew she would never buy that. Even if it had been, there was no paying off Jimmy Jambalaya. “I don’t know exactly how the quilt is going to help us,” he said. “It’s hard to explain.”

“Try me.”

Martin sighed.

How could he explain his grandmothers to her? Oh, he could tell her how both women had a touch of the oracle about them and had been sought for their wisdom and advice, back in the old country. Why would she believe it, though? Worse yet, how could he convince her that they had predicted this very day over thirteen years ago and had prepared for it? At least, he hoped.

*“Keep it close to you, for you will require it,”* they had said. Fat lot of good he’d been at following directions.

“I don’t think I can explain it, baby. I just have to find it. It’s all I have left.”

“Or we could run!”

Melissa looked as though she was about to pass over the threshold of emotional containment. She leaned against the wall.

“I’m sorry,” he said. “Please… just run. Run while you can.”

“Can’t,” Melissa said. “I have to help you find this chest.”

Martin had first seen the chest on his $20^{th}$ birthday. He had come home from college for the weekend, but awakened to an astounding sight. There in the main kitchen of his father's house were both of his grandmothers, patiently waiting to feed him his birthday breakfast. The sight of them together—two women, who had spat at the mere mention of one another for decades—was so jarring that he'd scarcely been able to speak. It felt as though his whole world had been turned inside out. Even more absurd was that after they had fed him his birthday breakfast, with a slice of the most amazing white cake for dessert, they had then presented him with a gift they had crafted *together*: a wooden chest, containing a quilt.

To explain this to Melissa would sound too simple and normal and grandmotherly. It would be impossible to convey the shock he had felt when his grandmothers had then, in perfect unbroken English, given him instructions as to the role their quilt would play in his life—in events that seemed to be happening *this very day.*

Martin soon found that his bedroom closet proved just as lacking in chests and quilts as the linen closet. Melissa had searched the guest room with the same result. He had no idea where to look next.

"You didn't throw it out, did you?" Melissa asked.

"Are you kidding?" he said. Even without his grandmothers' warning, he would never have thrown it out. Of course, he couldn't rule out having given it to Rachel at some point, or of her simply taking it. Both grandmothers were dead by the time she turned twenty.

The only thing they had left her was some old jewelry that she didn't like.

"What about a crawlspace?" Melissa asked.

"No."

"Attic, then?"

Martin almost said no, but stopped. *The attic!* Why hadn't he thought of the attic before? He had stored a bunch of old stuff up there when he first moved into the house. He couldn't recall what, off the top of his head, but it was worth a shot.

The door to the attic was set into the ceiling of the hallway, just outside the bathroom. The high ceilings were one of the main reasons he'd chosen the house. They did, however, make the attic door difficult to reach and more difficult to climb through. Unlike some he'd seen, though, this attic did not have a fold-down ladder for easy access.

For a moment he almost convinced himself that his memory of the attic might have been manufactured out of desperation. But, no, he remembered having to borrow a step-ladder from his neighbor across the street, Mr. Benci. He'd meant to buy one of his own, but had never gotten around to it.

"I'm going to need a chair," he told Melissa. She ran to the kitchen and returned dragging one of the chairs. Standing on it, he could just reach the attic door. His fingers fumbled at the painted metal latch that held the door in place. It was stiff, but he managed to turn it, allowing the door to drop down. It nearly struck him on the top of the head. Dry air poured from the dark space above him. There was no good way to climb into it, though, even from the chair.

"Here," Melissa said, standing on the floor with her back to him. She leaned forward and put her hands on her knees. "Step onto my back and I can help boost you up."

"Are you sure?"

"Yeah. At this point, a slipped disc is the least of our worries."

It took a couple of attempts to get his footing right, but Melissa's plan worked like a charm. With his foot on her back, she lifted him to within a hand hold of the attic door and he was able to pull himself up and through.

The air in the attic was hot and smelled of decay. There was a dead bird or a mouse up there somewhere, he reckoned. All he could see at first were shadows and angled beams of light from vents in the eaves. As he sat up, a string brushed his face and he realized it was the cord for the bare light bulb mounted to the side of a rafter. He pulled it and the bulb came to life, casting a dim light. Around him was a ten-foot section of plank flooring surrounded by a sea of pink insulation between ceiling joists. There were some cardboard boxes stacked at the far edge of the flooring. At first, Martin thought that was all that was there. Then, around the edge of the furthermost box, silhouetted against the light from the eaves, he saw a small dark shape. Martin scrambled for it, pushing away the boxes to reveal a simple wooden chest, about two feet in width with a foot of height and depth. It was carved from a dark-stained wood and bound with black metal bands.

"Is it there?" Melissa called.

"Yeah… Yeah, it is."

He picked the chest up. It was heavier than he remembered, and the metal bands were cool to the touch. In fact, the air around the box itself seemed cooler than it should have been in such a hot Virginia attic. He carried it into the light near the attic door and set it on the boards.

This was the moment of truth, for in all the years that he had owned the chest, its latch had never been opened; not since the day his grandmothers had placed the folded quilt inside and closed its lid.

His fingers found the latch. With a silent prayer, he pressed it with his thumb. It slid fluidly to one side, as though it had been freshly oiled that morning. It didn't even make a sound.

Martin lifted the lid of the chest and the dim bare bulb above him shone down onto the neatly folded rectangle of quilt that fit perfectly inside. He had not laid eyes on it in thirteen years, though he had occasionally seen it in dreams. Martin lifted it from its nest and began to unfold it. The back of the quilt was the dark blue of ocean depths. It was sewn through the padding to the quilt top in odd non-repeating patterns in red and gold thread. They looked like symbols, he realized. Martin turned the quilt, revealing its decorative top. There, stitched into the 144 squares of fabric that composed its surface, were the cloth illustrations his grandmothers had used in their tales. All the characters were there, from the dashing young Sparrow Salvatore, to the beautiful Natale with her ever-present ruby close around her neck, to the farmers and villagers of the clan army, and even the dark warriors and their cat-beasts, cut from black velvet. Scanning the quilt from the upper left corner all the way to the lower right, he could see the entire story of his ancestors played out in 6"x6" panels.

There were words stitched into some of the panels near the center of the quilt. They were stitched in the same gold and red thread as the quilt back, across darker fabrics, causing the words to stand out in the light, as though glowing from within. The words formed phrases in the same dialect exclusively used by his grandmothers, except for on his 20$^{th}$ birthday. Martin didn't understand all the words and noted that even some of the Italian that he recognized had been spelled out phonetically.

Alternating between the text panels were cloth illustrations of Natale reading from a book, Natale in the presence of a dark warrior, then of Natale riding to Sparrow Salvatore's rescue with an army of the warriors and their cat-beasts at her command. And in each of these illustrative panels, there were stitched more gold and red symbols.

Through the eaves, Martin heard the sound of a car pulling into the driveway. It traveled all the way to the top and stopped directly in front of the garage door. The engine died and there came the sound of a number of doors opening and closing.

"Martin, I think he's here," Melissa said from below.

*"Keep it close to you, for you will require it. When the day of your greatest need arrives, you must take it in your hands and voice the call of old. Only then will the name of our families be restored."*

Martin closed his eyes and took a breath. Then he looked upon the face of the quilt and, in a low tone, gave voice to the words he found there.

"Martin, they're at the door," Melissa said from below. He tried to ignore her, but this became more difficult when he heard the sounds of laughter from outside followed by three very persistent knocks at his front door.

He continued to read.

"Hey, Marty, looks like we're early," Jimmy Jambalaya's voice called through the eaves.

Martin could feel beads of sweat trickling down his back, and then from his hairline into his eyebrows. He wanted to wipe it away, but he needed both hands to hold the quilt.

Three more knocks.

"I don't think he's home, boys," Jimmy said. "Let's go get a beer." There was more laughter.

"I think someone's at the back door, too," Melissa whispered from the hall. Martin felt a flush of anger at this. He wanted to scream at her to run and hide, but he couldn't. He couldn't even whisper it because he somehow knew that if he didn't finish the words without interruption he would either have to start over or get no second chance at all.

"Does the doorbell work?" Tino said. "I keep pressing the button, but I don't hear nothing inside."

"We better knock harder then," Jimmy said.

There was a beat and then something large smashed against the front door. Martin nearly lost his place. More sweat tipped out of his eyebrows, a bead of which ran into his left eye.

"Not polite to keep us waiting, Marty," Jimmy said. There was more laughter from the other men and the sound of Jimmy's favored Bren Ten being cocked. "He is still in there, right?" Jimmy asked, an edge to his voice.

"Oh, he's in there, all right," Tino said. "His girl's in there, too."

This brought a burst of vile laughter from Jimmy.

There was another try at smashing the front door. It held.

Martin continued to read, but he desperately wanted to know where Melissa was hiding. He couldn't hear her talking anymore so he hoped she had gone to hide, but the need to look through the attic door to confirm this nearly overwhelmed him. He paused, then changed his mind. Scanning the line he had been reading, nothing on it looked familiar. He was almost afraid to even think the words he saw. Then he saw the word he had left off with: s*ervitude.* He took a breath and started reading again with the words after it.

"… in cambio…del vostro… alegianse."

Martin's eyes dropped to the next row, but there were no gold and red letters to be seen there. He quickly looked over the entire bottom half of the quilt, but other than the occasional symbol in gold, there were no more words. Had he finished?

Below there was another strike against the door.

Martin looked around him. Nothing seemed to have happened. Had he done something wrong? Had he mispronounced a word? More words? This didn't make sense. Then, a horrible thought occurred to him: what if his grandmothers were simply crazy old women who'd made it all up?

Another strike, this time accompanied by the splintering of wood and the pained grunt of whichever thug Jimmy had ordered to break down the door. Jimmy would soon be inside.

Martin threw down the quilt and dropped his head through the attic door. Both Melissa and the chair were gone from the hallway. However, the attic door still hung down limply. With the latch on the other side, there was no good way to pull it up and make it stay. He hoped Jimmy and his thugs wouldn't notice it right away. He might have time to find something stout with which to smash the first head that poked through the attic door. Maybe he could at least brain Jimmy with the chest itself. Martin reached for the chest, then noticed that both of his arms had broken out in goose flesh.

Something in the corner of his vision moved above the center of the attic's floorboards. He moved his head to see what it was but saw only a shape. This was the only way his brain could define what he was seeing—a tall black shape with glints of red in it and of another color that Martin couldn't readily identify. He couldn't even identify the shape of the shape. It was as if his brain couldn't translate what his eyes were seeing. And while he could detect no facial features within the shape, he had the distinct impression that it was looking at him. The entire attic was suddenly frigid.

Below, the door burst open and large men filed into his house.

"Find the girl," Jimmy said. "Find them both."

Martin barely heard any of this. He was too busy concentrating on the whispery sounds he was hearing in his head. The sounds hurt.

The shape in the corner began to change, growing tendrils of blackness. One of these lashed out suddenly and touched Martin's forehead before he could even flinch away. The tendril withdrew into the still hazy mass, which began to shift again, coalescing into something else. Then, as though his brain were finally able to translate his vision, the shape resolved into a tall, thick man in a black leather overcoat. The coat appeared scaly and wet. Beneath it, the shape wore a three-piece suit with pinstripes of exactly the color Martin could not identify before. There was a tall fedora situated low above a meaty, bulbous-nosed face that, strangely, Martin recognized. It took him a few seconds before it hit him: the man looked like Luca Brasi, a character from the movie *The Godfather.* Martin couldn't place the name of the actor who played Luca Brasi off the top of his head, but whatever it was that stood across the attic from him now was a double of Don Corleone's enforcer. Only his clothing looked like Hollywood's idea of a gangster from the '30s. Even in the face of the man's odd appearance, Martin knew that he was staring at one of the dark warriors from his grandmothers' tales.

The warrior looked at his surroundings. Then words whispered in Martin's head, saying:

*'this plane... again'*

The words still hurt, but at least they were in English.

The warrior stared at him. Martin didn't really know what to say to it. He had only been given the words to bring it here, not the words to say afterward.

*'you are... the Salvatore?'*

"Um, ah, yes," Martin said, squinting in discomfort. "My middle name is Salvatore. Martin Salvatore Riscili. I am the... uh, the Salvatore."

"Yeah, I heard it too," someone said from the hall below.

Martin realized he had spoken louder than intended. He held his breath and became very aware of the creaky boards beneath his feet.

"Marty? Where arrre youuuuu?" Jimmy called. He said something else too, but it was drowned out by the words of the warrior.

*'the Salvatore requires... assistance?'*

"Yes. Assistance, yes," Martin said, whispering. He pointed toward the attic door. "Those men are here to kill me."

Then, in an audible voice that reminded Martin less of Luca Brasi and more of sharpened icicles, the warrior said, "Death?"

"Yes, *death*. Of me. I don't want it," Martin said. He felt like he was talking to an immigrant fresh off the boat. He supposed he was.

The warrior did not actually smile, but there was something about his face that seemed pleased all the same. "We understand death."

From directly below the attic door, Martin heard Tino's voice say, "Hey, Jimmy, look." Martin could just imagine him pointing at the open square in the ceiling and then Jimmy taking several seconds to make the deduction of what the open attic door meant.

"Ohh, look there boys," Jimmy said, right on time, three long Mississippis later. "I think we got us a little birdy up in the attic."

Tino laughed. "He's got the air on up there, too. Feel the draft?"

"Cold birdy," Jimmy said. "Who wants to hear the birdy sing?"

At least four other voices said variations on "I do!"

Martin shoved the quilt chest over the edge of the attic door with his foot. It fell and made a satisfying wet crunch as it struck. Tino's distinctive tenor voice groaned in pain just before his fleshy bulk hit the floor.

"Aw, shit, Marty," Jimmy said. "You shouldn't have done that."

Martin jumped away from the attic door as two bullets sang through the boards near it, sending chunks of wood into the air. The gunshots themselves made little sound. Jimmy's crew must have come prepared with silencers.

The warrior's Luca Brasi jaw twitched, like that of a cat stalking prey.

"The Salvatore requires protection?" it said.

"Yes! Protection!" Martin shouted. "I need protection right now!"

More bullets burst through the boards, closer to where Martin stood. Jimmy and his men were firing randomly into the ceiling of the hall and bathroom. Chips of wood were blasted in all directions. Clouds of dust billowed through the growing number of sunbeams left by bullets exiting the roof.

"And the terms?" the warrior said.

"Terms? What terms?"

Martin stepped out onto the joists above the guest bedroom, out of the current line of fire. The warrior was not so lucky. Two bullets ripped through his body, leaving twin trails of hazy darkness, one from his leathery right shoulder and the other from the top of his hat. The warrior didn't seem at all bothered by the wounds. His only acknowledgment of them came as the dark trails pulled back in on themselves, plugging the holes with ebony scabs. The whispers in Martin's head returned.

*'in your summons... you agreed to our terms... this is your intention?'*

"What terms?" Martin shouted.

*'we shall assist you... we shall ally with you... we shall protect you...'*

"But we get a cut," it said aloud.

The bullets had stopped now, but Martin could hear the men reloading below.

"Let's see if the little bird's still singing now," Jimmy said. "Gimme a boost."

There were sounds of struggle below as Jimmy Jambalaya tried to haul his fat frame onto the shoulders of whichever henchman was the tallest. They seemed to be having limited success, but it would only be a matter of time before they either succeeded or it occurred to them to go find a chair.

Martin looked into the warrior's eyes. "I accept the terms," he said.

The warrior's expression returned to the one of amusement from before.

When Jimmy Jambalaya's head did finally poke through the attic door, he seemed almost surprised to find Martin still alive, balancing in a crouch on the joists.

"Hi there, little bird," Jimmy said with a yellow grin. That grin vanished an instant later as he noticed the warrior. Martin had no idea how Jimmy perceived the warrior, but if it was anything like his own perception, the warrior had lost his human shape and become something more akin to a gigantic leathery panther, with eyes of a color he couldn't name.

The shape leapt across the attic and had its mouth around Jimmy's head before the man could even scream. Then the shape was gone, having slithered through the comparatively tiny attic door, taking the rest of Jimmy with him. There followed gunfire as well as sounds of running and a series of five screams that were each, in turn, brought to a cold silence.

Nearly a minute passed before Martin could bring himself to move from his place on the ceiling joists. He crawled to the edge of the attic door, being careful of the bullet-weakened floor there. Something wet lay on the boards, but he was able to avoid it as he lowered himself through the opening and dropped to the floor, twisting his ankle.

All was now quiet in the house. The bodies of his father's former coworkers were nowhere to be found. There was some blood, but not as much as he would have expected from the sounds he had heard. There was also no sign of either the warrior or its cat-shape.

"Mel?" Martin called. "Melissa?" There was no reply, though now he did hear a sound from the bedroom. Limping on his newly-injured leg, Martin moved down the hallway until he came to his open bedroom door. Melissa wasn't there. Instead, standing at the threshold of Martin's closet, facing into it, was the warrior, back in something approximating Luca Brasi in his '30s pinstripe, though the resemblance was no longer exact.

"Mel?" Martin called.

*'alliance... assistance... protection,'* the warrior said in his head. *'it is good to again... be on this... plane'*

The warrior turned to look at Martin. There was a red gleam in its eye that Martin didn't like.

"Where is Melissa?" he said.

“Terms,” the warrior said aloud in his sharpened icicle voice. “Our cut. You have… kicked upstairs.”

It smiled.

*‘protection’*

Martin collapsed onto his bedroom carpet and screamed into his hands, causing the warrior’s mobster shape to flicker with each new sob of emotion. The warrior waited for Martin to finish, then reached down and gently touched his shoulder.

*‘who do you want us to kill next?’*

# ...to a Flame

It was a cool West Virginia summer evening and the wife and I had just finished a late supper of her famous steak & stinkers—meaning to say, cube steak, fried ramps and beans. The sun was starting to set over the hills behind us, turning the mountains to the east purple and casting a glow over the whole valley. We'd retired to the porch to enjoy a beer, with our feet propped up on the rusty old deep freeze that I still ain't gotten round to getting rid of. It seemed a natural setting in which to open discussions for where our Saturday evening might lead us. We were part way into negotiations when we were interrupted, mid-smooch, by the grind of half-bald tires on the gravel road. I saw the yellow door panel on the otherwise red Dodge pick-up and knew it was Virgil Hawks pulling up.

"Evening, Virgil," I said as he staggered up the walk. "What brings you out this...?" My voice dropped off as I caught sight of Virgil's face. It was ghost white and held an expression of what I can only describe as pants-filling terror.

"Hell, Virgil. What's wrong?"

"Jeff, I'm in trouble something fierce. Evenin' Marsha," he said, touching the bill of his cap to my wife with one hand. His other hand held the stub of a cigarette.

"Can't be all that bad, Virg."

"Oh, yes it can."

"Well, okay then. Come on up and tell us about it."

Virgil scratched at the back of his sandy-colored head. "No. I'd rather not. I think you best come out to the truck, Jeff. Something you probably ought to see."

I shrugged an apology in Marsha's direction for my untimely departure from negotiations. Not having much use for Virgil, she frowned and went in the house while I followed him on out to the drive.

Virgil popped open the tailgate of his Dodge. An old tarp in the truck bed was covering something big and lumpy. He pulled back the edge of it.

"Well, I'll be, Virgil. You've got a dead mothman in the back of your truck."

It looked like a mothman to me, at least; the very sort they had trouble with up in Point Pleasant some years back. It was grayish black, about the size of man with legs like a man's but with leathery-looking wings for arms. It didn't have hair or fur, but looking closer I could see it was covered in some kind of narrow flat scales, about an inch long. They weren't feathers, but weren't too far from it—like someone's strange idea of alien feather-hair. Not sure why they call these things mothmen. Didn't look like any moth I'd ever seen. More like a big, ugly, squashed bat that's missing a head on account of its blood-red eyes being set into its chest, like. Those red eyes were part way closed, but I could see there was no life left in them.

"Yup, I'd say that's a dead mothman, all right."

"No shit, Jeff? Really? Cause I thought maybe it was a deer!"

"Now, Virgil, there's no call for sarcasm. Just calm down."

"Calm down?" Virgil said, tossing his lanky arms in the air. "I got a dead mothman in the back of my truck and you want me to *calm down*? This ain't some poached cow we're talking about, Jeff. It's a goddamn alien creature. Or, at the very least, some kind of pan-dimensional being."

"I understand, Virgil, but getting all excited's not gonna help anything at this point, now is it?"

Virgil's horse face glared at me in the dwindling light. He took a drag on what remained of his cigarette, then tossed it aside. He tapped another out of an almost full pack of Marlboro Reds and made several attempts to light it with a match before his shaky hands succeeded. I didn't want to rile him up any more, so I didn't point out that he was supposed to have given up the coffin-nails for good, months ago.

"Whoo, it sure does stink," I said. "Smells like a rancid turnip fart. Where'd you say you found it?"

"I didn't find it. I shot it."

"You shot it?"

"Yeah," Virgil said. He looked embarrassed. "I thought it was a coyote."

I looked at the big, dead, red-eyed, squashed bat-thing in the truck bed. "You thought *that* was a coyote?"

Virgil blinked. "I told you last week I thought there was coyotes coming up on my property? Remember?" I didn't remember, but I nodded anyway. Virgil always thinks something is sneaking around his house and stirring up his dogs. If it ain't coyotes, it's mountain lions or rabid ground hogs or somebody out to bust in his shed and steal his prized but practically antique welding torch. How he expects me to keep up with it all, I don't know. "Well, a couple hours ago, I thought I heard one of them out behind the tool shed," Virgil said. "I could hear it back there, scratching around in the dirt. So I got my rifle and crept up to the corner of the shed to see if I could surprise it. Only when I whipped around the corner, it was *this* thing, all bent over with its back to me. I think it was taking a shit."

"So you shot it?"

"It was dim."

"Dim? It's barely dim *now* and it's near eight-thirty."

"I'm telling you it was dim, dammit! I thought it might attack."

"While it was taking a shit?"

"Confound it, Jeff! You ain't helping!"

I could tell that Virgil was on the edge of losing all good sense, if he hadn't already fallen off. I figured I'd better play along.

"All right, all right. So it was dim, you thought you saw a big black flappy-winged coyote having a squat behind the tool shed and you shot it. Them's the facts?"

Virgil frowned at me, but nodded.

"Okay. What are you going do with it now that it's dead?"

"I'm getting the hell rid of it is what I'm doing."

"What for? Why not sell it? Tabloids pay big money for pictures of aliens and bigfoots and stuff. What you think the *National Enquirer*'d give you for the real live… well, the real dead McCoy?"

"Are you crazy? I can't keep this thing! I can't let nobody know I've even seen it."

"Why not?"

"Don't you know anything, Jeff?" Then he dropped his voice down to a whisper and said, "M.I.B.s."

"M.I.B.s?"

"The Men In Black. Them government guys what watches out for aliens."

"Aw, hell! Here it comes," I said, rolling my eyes. "You been listening to all the crazy folks calling in to *Rik Winston's UFO All Night Show* again. Haven't you?" If there's one thing Virgil loves, it's listening to kooks on the radio spouting about alien abductions and cattle mutilations and anal probes.

"It ain't crazy, Jeff, it's…"

"No, wait. If I recall, this is the same show that claimed the United Nations is run by vampire-witch-aliens who're trying to take over the country and get rid of daylight savings time? Same show, right?"

"Jeff, just shut up and listen. This is important," Virgil said.

"Fine."

"So, like I was trying to say… Rik had on this doctor guy who says he saw an alien. Said he was out hiking in the woods and stumbled up on one."

"One of these things?"

"No, one of them gray ones with the big black eyes."

"Did it *probe* him?"

"No. It up and killed his dog, though."

"His dog?"

Virgil sighed. "Yes, his dog! He was walking his dog in the woods, they found an alien, the alien up and kills the dog and the doctor guy got mad and whacked it in the head with a stick."

"The alien?"

"Yes, the alien," Virgil said. "The doctor guy hits it and thinks it's dead, but he doesn't know what to do with it. So he takes the alien home and puts it in his deep freeze. But first, he takes pictures of it. I seen them on Rik's website."

"See, there you go. Pictures. He probably sold 'em for a million bucks, too."

"That's just it. He didn't get the chance."

Virgil peered around at the tree-line, as if there might be a *Man in Black* there, listening.

"Couple days later, somebody breaks in and ransacks the guy's house when he was gone and steals the alien out of the deep freeze!"

"Uh huh."

"Then the threatening phone calls start and big black cars trying to run him down on the highway. The whole bit. He had to leave town for good. Now he's on the run from the Men in Black full time. He calls in to Rik's show every few months with an update—from a different and undisclosed location."

"Men in Black, huh?"

"Hell, yeah!" Virgil said. "And these guys ain't nice, like the ones in the movies. They'll kill you, Jeff. They'll hunt you down if it hare-lips Georgia. And they'll make it look like an accident."

"Well, that sounds real bad for this doctor guy," I said.

"Bad for him and bad for me. MIB's, man… They can detect the aliens with sensors and stuff and they come down real hard on any witnesses. Soon as I realized what I'd shot, I drug the sumbitch to the truck and covered it up quick. Lord!"

"Heh. You'd better count yourself lucky you didn't wing one of them big ass Flatwoods monsters. You'd never have even got it in the truck in the first place."

"Oh, ha, ha, Jeff! You think this is a joke?"

"Now, Virgil," I said, nearly laughing at the thought of Virgil trying to use an engine-block crane to hoist a giant alien wearing a skirt off the ground. Flatwoods monsters always were the damnedest looking things. "I'm sorry. It's not a joke."

"Damn straight it's not," Virgil said. He propped his leg up on the edge of the tailgate and set about seriously smoking the last of his cigarette. "They say just seeing one of these things is a harbinger of doom."

"How you figure?"

Virgil gave me a long disgusted look. "Damn, Jeff. I know you're averse to reading anything but the word of God, but you ain't read *the* textbook about the mothman? *The Mothman Prophecies*?"

"Nah. Saw the movie. Pretty damn weird, if you ask me. Not bad acting for Richard Gere, though. And that whassername… blond actress."

"Laura Linney?"

"Yeah, that's the one. I like her. Still, it pissed me off that they never showed you what the damn mothman looked like. How you supposed to have a good monster movie and not even *show* the monster?"

"Well, you can forget all the weird stuff in the movie 'cause most of it didn't really happen like that. But that thing at the end, when the bridge collapsed and all those people died?"

"Yeah?"

"Well, there you go! There's your horrible tragedy, harbinged by the mothman."

"Is it, now?"

"Sure thing."

I waited a few seconds for Virgil to follow this up, but he just stood there looking smug. I was sure I'd regret it, but I asked how he figured this to be true.

"You got to pay attention, Jeff. You got to look at the big picture. See, folks around Point Pleasant had been seeing UFOs and M.I.B.s and the mothman for a whole year. Some of them were having horrible dreams, too. Even dreams about the bridge collapsing. Then, after it did collapse, poof—no more mothman."

"Uh huh."

"I'm just saying it ain't good to see one now. It's a foretelling of bad stuff about to happen. To me, even!"

"Seems to me that if the mothman could foretell bad stuff happening, it might've foretold a little for itself. Maybe then it would've chose a place to squat where it was less likely to get shot in the ass."

I expected Virgil to be mad at me for joking around again, but this time he looked plum hurt.

"I don't know why I thought you'd be any help. I don't know why I even came out here in the first place."

"Well, I don't, either," I said. "I don't see why you didn't dump your horrible monster off Milton Cliff like you would any other carcass?"

Virgil fixed me with a penetrating stare. "And just how do you know I dump carcasses off Milton Cliff?"

"Oh, please. Everyone around here, up to and including the game warden, knows you dump there. Especially when what you're dumping ain't in season."

"Exactly."

"What?"

"Exactly," Virgil repeated. "As in, there you go."

I realized that Virgil was actually making a point here. A damn good point, too. Everybody *did* know of Virgil's relationship to Milton Cliff. In fact, I knew fellows who dumped out-of-season carcasses there to put the blame in Virgil's direction. Anything odd got dumped there, all fingers would point back to him.

"All right," I said. "Why not dump it someplace else then?"

"Ain't you seen police shows, Jeff? They could trace my bullet back to me, no problem. Even if I dug it out first, they could examine the microbes and trajectories and what have you. I'd be cooked. No, this thing's got to be hid or destroyed for good. We're talking about a mothman, here, Jeff. This ain't some old deep freeze you can roll into a holler and forget about. This thing has got to be..."

Virgil stopped. His mouth hung open there for a bit, then grew wide and broke into a grin. I thought this was very odd, until I realized he wasn't staring at me any more—he was looking back toward the porch. Before I could even get all the way turned around, I knew what he was grinning about: that old rusted-out deep freeze that had been a moldering away on my porch for months now.

"Let me ask you something, Jeff. When you're out hunting and you come across an old fridge down in a holler, you ever stop to take a look inside it?"

"Hell no. Never can tell what kind of nasty thing somebody might have left in it."

"Yeah. Same here," Virgil said. Then his grin widened even further. "Course, wouldn't nobody be able to look in it at all if we welded it shut first."

"Strictly for safety's sake," I said smiling back. "Can't have kids playing in it, after all. Somebody could get hurt."

"There you go," Virgil said. "I'll go get my torch."

While Virgil drove home to get his welding torch, I went inside to tell Marsha the good news. Of course, I didn't mention the part about the mothman, since she wouldn't cotton to having such things up near the house. But she was pretty happy about Virgil finally helping me get rid of that old freezer. We almost had to restart our night's negotiations, but held off on account of Virgil's expected return.

A couple hours passed by, though, and Virgil still hadn't come back. I began to worry. Turns out, I had good reason.

The fire department never did figure out for sure what caused the explosion that destroyed Virgil's tool shed and truck. Oh, they brought in investigators and inspectors and what have you, but they never figured it out. Not for sure. The popular notion was that Virgil had lit up a cigarette in the shed, igniting fumes from a leak in the gas tanks of his welding torch.

Maybe so.

Trouble is, they never found Virgil's body. Nary a trace of it. Nor of any other bodies. Especially not ones that looked like a big squashed bat—I think that sort of thing might have made the paper.

I also thought it was odd how the coroner had Virgil declared dead right away. His point was that nothing could have survived an explosion like that. I tried to press the issue, pointing out that Virgil might not have been in that explosion, but he didn't seem to want to hear it. Virgil was staying dead and that was that.

Can't say I much enjoy summer evenings anymore. Oh, I still like to sit in the porch swing. And I still prop my feet up on the rusty old deep freeze that I still ain't got around to dumping. I can't do it, though, without thinking of Virgil.

If I'm honest with myself, I reckon he probably is dead. If not from the explosion then from *other* causes that I don't like to think about. Most days, I prefer to imagine that Virgil had a change of heart on his way home that night. Maybe he felt bad about getting me involved in something he thought was so dangerous. Maybe he went home and blew up his own shed, faked his death and slipped away into the night.

I like to think he's still out there somewhere. That he's moving from state to state, or even country to country, living by his wits, on the run from the Men in Black full time. I've even been known to tune in to *Rik Winston's UFO All Night Show.* I keep hoping Virgil will phone in from a different and undisclosed location to update the listeners on his adventures.

So far, though, he never has.

# Wolves Among Stones at Dusk

Atop the low mesa, in the scorched-orange glow of the setting Arizona sun, a Mexican Gray Wolf paced in frustration. Few humans have ever seen a member of this rarest of North American species of wolves, fewer still have ever heard one growl, and fewer than that could claim to have heard the gurgle of hunger pangs coming from the stomach of such a creature. The man seated on the edge of the mesa's cliff, a few feet away from the wolf, might have been able to accomplish all three of these rare feats, had he only been paying attention.

The wolf sat in the old man's shadow, eyeing his form silhouetted against the sunset. Even squinting against the light, the wolf could see the long and stringy gray fur of his quarry as it fluttered in the breeze of dusk. Similarly caught in the breeze were the strings and ribbons of the torn fabric that still covered the man's body. Dozens of growing shadows also stretched out from the many paw prints that this wolf and his pack brothers had left in the dust of the rock shelf over the past months.

The senses of wolves are fine-tuned receptors of many levels of information broadcast by their prey. They can tell, for instance, when an animal is wounded by the rhythm of its breathing. They can savor the delicious aroma of fear and know from it precisely when their prey is about to bolt. The old man, however, gave off almost no such information. It frustrated the wolf, for as little as his senses registered about the man, he might as well have been staring at a blank patch of air. The only emotion he or any of his pack brothers had ever been able to sense from him was an occasional flicker of regret. They didn't recognize this as having any significance, however; regret being an emotion alien to wolves of any species. While the lines of the man's face indicated age, there was something about him that made the wolf certain this human was far older than he appeared. The wolf could smell the old man's blood—even beneath the layers of grit that coated his pale skin, but its flow was almost imperceptible.

The wolf listened. After nearly a minute, he heard the beat of the man's heart, the stir of his blood, and then silence once more. This was wrong, the wolf knew. All animals were creatures of blood. Blood was life—and life, by right, belonged to the wolves to take as they pleased, or as they dared. A creature whose life did not flow even as fast as that of the hated hardshells was not a natural creature. However, as the wolf had long ago reasoned, it *was* still blood. This old man—whose blood refused to flow properly, whose skin refused to rend beneath fang, whose bones refused to break when, in impotent rage, he and his pack brothers had toppled the man's body from the edge of the cliff—was a continuing puzzle in the wolf's mind. His pack brothers had all but given up, but the puzzle was what brought the wolf back to the top of the mesa nearly every day. The wolf's own chipped teeth served as an ever-present reminder that this bizarre prey had not yet been caught, despite the fact that he had also never fled.

Padding two steps closer across the still scorching surface of the dusty mesa, the wolf allowed himself a whine of irritation. His impulse was to rush at the man, to bound off of the muscles of his back and send his body over the edge again. At barely seven cactuses in height it was not a long fall to the desert floor below; but to investigate the fallen form would have required a journey back along the mesa, to where the treacherously steep and rocky face gave way to a more easily traversable slope. Making the journey would be a fruitless waste of energy, for, as always, he would find the old man lying at the foot of the mesa, his body still bent in its seated position, unharmed save for fresh rips in his fabric covering. The old man might remain there, undisturbed for days or even weeks, until he would one day again be found seated on the edge of the mesa's cliff, his narrowed blue eyes staring into the distance, his face timeworn like that of the mesa itself. None of his brothers had ever observed the man making the return journey to his perch. They had never seen any indication of movement from him at all. Clearly, though, he could move when it suited him to do so.

One of his pack brothers, Fungus, claimed to have once seen an old woman on the mesa as well. Fungus claimed she had emerged from what he described as a wood-lined hole in the air and that she had carried a shiny stick. None of his other brothers had witnessed this and none of them would admit that they did not know what a hole in the air meant. Fungus was crazy.

The wolf remained seated a few tail lengths distance from the old man and waited as the evening grew darker. Prey of a more animated nature would be stirring before long and the wolf knew that his hunger would soon be sated.

In the distance, across the dry lake bed overlooked by the mesa, there came a humming, growling sound. Within a short time, two lights appeared to accompany the sound and the wolf knew that this signaled the approach of one of the long, armored, round-legged beasts that had been tamed by the humans. The wolf had seen such beasts before, but their territory was usually limited to the long stretches of black rock the humans had arranged on the far side of the lakebed. On occasion, however, the humans and their beasts had strayed into his pack's territory. The wolf knew that he must be on his guard for moving humans were less predictable than the still old man.

As the long beast came closer, the wolf could see that it was black and with two fins at its rear, much like the fishes he had seen rushing through the distant rivers in the rainy season. It stopped moving some distance from the foot of the mesa, perhaps not wishing to venture close to some of the larger rocks that had fallen from its face. The beast stopped growling, but light continued to pour from its eyes. Presently the beast's black armored flanks opened, causing a low buzzing sound that only ceased when two humans had emerged from each side of the beast and again closed its flanks. The wolf could at once smell their sweat and then their blood. It was pumping just fine. Then the humans began to make their usual noises.

One of them, a tall lanky man whose form, the wolf observed, might lend itself to swiftness, struck the side of the armored beast with his foot. To the wolf's senses, the man blazed with anger and sweat.

The other man was taller and stouter than the lanky man. He responded in plaintive tones, his paws held out. The wolf couldn't understand his sounds, but thought the big man could prove to be powerful, if slow prey.

The lanky man blazed again, which in turn sent up a flash of anger from the big man, which ebbed though remained. Then the lanky man reached into his clothing and produced a small white stick. His paw then seemed to catch fire and he touched the tip of the stick into the flames until smoke began to puff from his mouth.

From his perch on the mesa, the wolf watched as the two men walked to the rear of their beast to open what must have been its armored, flat tail. The bigger man reached into the rectum of the beast and, with some effort, withdrew from it another human. For a moment, the wolf entertained the notion that the humans were born from their armored beasts. Then he became distracted by the new sensory combination of sweat, blood and, most deliciously, fear, as the newly born man was dropped to the ground. It took a moment to see the new man clearly, but his top legs appeared to be bound behind his back and his lower legs bound at the feet. The bound man smelled younger than the first two men, scarcely older than a pup, but he wasn't a small man, either. Another growl of hunger escaped from the stomach of the wolf and he padded closer to the edge of the cliff, watching as the big man looped his paws into the pits of the bound man's top legs and pulled him along the desert floor and into the light of the beast's eyes. The lanky man followed and propped one of his leather-covered lower paws onto the beast's lip. He puffed out more smoke and made triumphant, gloating noises. The lanky man's anger, however, remained in flow.

The bound man on the ground made noises through the covering around his jaws. The lanky man laughed loudly at this. The big man laughed as well, but there was fear behind it instead of mirth.

The bound man made an aggressive sound from beneath his mouth covering. The lanky man flashed with anger and struck out with one of his lower paws, connecting with the bound man's midsection. This elicited a muffled groan of pain.

The lanky man reached one of his paws into the back of his leg-coverings and returned with something heavy and black. The bound man instantly began making louder, more frantic sounds. His heart was racing. Fear was pouring out of him, causing the wolf's mouth to water. He wished his pack brothers were nearby. Together, they might have a chance of catching at least two of these men before any of them could hide in the flanks or rectum of their armored beast. After frustrated months of wondering what an easy human meal might taste like, this opportunity was tantalizing.

The lanky man began to make louder sounds, drowning out the pleading noises of the bound man. The noises went on at length until the bound man thrashed his body again, striking out with one of his back legs, which had apparently come free of its binding. The lanky man dodged out of the way, scarcely avoiding the strike and the bound man's foot connected with the lip of the armored beast instead. The armored beast did not cry out.

The lanky man raged at the big man, his fire stick falling from his mouth, the heavy black thing waving in his paw. The big man became a mixture of fear, anger, and what seemed to the wolf like a far, far smaller amount of that bizarre, alien emotion he had occasionally sensed from the old man.

The wolf moved to the very edge of the mesa's cliff. He could see the bound man still thrashing on the ground, rolling partially out of the beast's eye lights. If it were half an hour later, the bound man would have rolled into pitch blackness, but in the twilight he could still be seen even by the humans. The wolf could smell the sweat and dirt that now caked the man's face, could practically see the blood roiling beneath the thin skin of his neck. He longed to sink his chipped fangs into that soft neck. Without his pack, though, he did not dare move. For now, he would stay upon the mesa, next to the stone-like old man, and observe.

The lanky man shouted below and waved his heavy black thing some more until the big man seemed to find his motion. He stepped around the edge of the armored beast, leaned over the bound man and struck down upon him with a clenched paw. The motion wasn't precisely quick, but it was powerful enough to still the movements of the bound man. The wolf could smell urine almost immediately, but the bound man's heart was still beating strong.

While the lanky man shouted, the big man walked to the tail of the armored beast and searched the ground in the lights from the beast's bowels until he located one of the bindings that had been on the bound man's legs. He returned to the beast's head and was bending over beyond it to where the bound man lay when the lanky man flushed with fury. The big man flashed fear as the lanky man waived his heavy black thing about. Then the lanky man quieted and turned the heavy black thing in his paw, holding it by its longer end. He held out the short end to the big man, who immediately pulsed with equal parts fear and revulsion.

The big man made a sound like a whimper. The lanky man bared his teeth. The wolf could smell smoke and the onions on his breath—pathetic plant-eaters. The wolf could feel the continued pulsing of the big man's nerves, and he began to make more plaintive sounds with his paws held up, not taking the offered black heavy thing.

The redness of the lanky man's anger darkened, and his tone became a low growl. He continued his growl for some time before his anger pulsed brightly at the end of his sounds, and he shoved the heavy black thing at the big man again. That was when a rock from the upper face of the mesa fell away beneath the wolf's position. It impacted noisily against the slight slope of the otherwise near-vertical face of the mesa. The wolf didn't know if his own weight had caused it to fall, but he could see that it had drawn the attention of the men on the desert floor. They had turned toward the sound and were holding their paws up to block the glare from the armored beast. While the sun had already set, the wolf knew there was possibly still enough light for even the humans to make out his shape and that of the old man. The wolf stood his ground.

The lanky man made low sounds, pointing toward the top of the mesa. He then walked to the open rectum of the armored beast and brought from it a short stick, the end of which burst into light like a smaller version of one of the eyes of the beast itself. He turned the beam of the stick's eye in the direction of the mesa until it came to rest upon the face of the old man. The old man's blue eyes remained narrowed and unmoving, staring into the distance at something only he seemed able to perceive. The wolf drew away from the beam, but his movement must have been noticed, for the beam quickly flicked into his own eyes.

The lanky man made more low noises. The big man joined him in this hushed song. Then the lanky man began to approach the mesa, his beam returning to the face of the old man. He began to make louder noises, his teeth bared in a grin, his tone bright and kindly. The tone, however, did not connect with the expression of the lanky man's eyes. The wolf could sense an undercurrent of nervousness and aggression beneath the cheer. He continued to make the friendly noises, gesturing behind him to the big man and to the armored beast as he moved slowly closer. Then he paused and moved his light beam from the old man's face down his seated body. He called something back to the big man, then darted the beam onto the wolf again. Then the lanky man brought the heavy black thing up just behind his light stick, and continued moving forward toward the face of the mesa. In the darkness, the lanky man tripped over one of the many loose stones that were in plentiful supply near the foot of the mesa and he stumbled forward, flailing his top legs to keep his balance. His light flickered down for a moment to check his footing, then on across the path before him. Within moments, though, he had returned his beam to the old man's face.

The big man made louder noises. He had moved midway between the armored beast and the face of the mesa, but he did not have a light stick of his own. The lanky man stopped moving at the sound and seethed, but didn't shift his beam from the old man's face. He called up to the old man in slow, soothing tones, but the wolf could see the threat of danger in the lanky man's eyes as he again raised his black heavy thing behind the light.

The black thing spat out three bursts of fire that sounded louder than thunderclaps. The wolf dropped into a startled crouch, but had already felt the vibrations as two of the fire bursts struck the face of the mesa below, sending more rock raining down. The third struck the old man's knee, rocking him on his perch, but doing no damage. Even the cloth covering of the man's legs was untouched, for it had been torn away during the many times the old man had been pushed from the mesa's cliff by his pack brothers.

Carefully, the wolf raised his head to see over the cliff. The lanky man was covering his face with one of his top legs against the shower of rock chips. Then his light shone again across the old man's unchanged face.

He called something back to the big man, who throbbed with confusion. The wolf could smell the big man's fear. And beyond the edge of the armored beast, the wolf could hear a low moaning from where the bound man lay.

The lanky man lifted the heavy black thing and it spat another burst of fire and noise. This time the fire burst struck the old man on the chin and bounced away into the sky. The old man rocked back from the force, balanced momentarily on the pivot of his rear, then he fell forward again into his seated position. Other than a small spot where the fire blast had chipped away some of the crust of sand and dust on the old man's chin, though, there was no sign that he'd been struck at all.

The big man shouted something in jubilant tones, pointing toward the old man. The lanky man, however, was furious. Now his pretense of cheer was completely gone and he moved closer to the mesa, moving out of the wolf's line of sight. The wolf crept slowly to the edge of the mesa's cliff and peered over it. An instant later, he was struck by the beam of light from the lanky man's stick. The wolf jerked his head back just before another thunder burst sounded, sending up a blast of rocks from the edge of the cliff. Then another burst followed, this one bouncing off of the old man's shoulder, spinning his body around slightly until his bent knees caught on the edge of the cliff.

Out of sight below, the lanky man screamed in rage. The light beam danced frantically across the old man's lower legs. There then followed a loud click and another angry cry from the lanky man.

The light vanished. The wolf couldn't see what was happening below, but from the sound of it he didn't need to see. He could hear the lanky man's steps as he moved back down the slope of the foot of the mesa followed by shouts back toward the big man. Even as he was making this noise, though, the wolf could hear the sound of rocks sliding beneath the man's back paws. The lanky man's heart rate increased as he flailed his top legs to compensate. More stones could be heard sliding as the man scrambled through them, and then there came a shout that ended abruptly as the lanky man's body struck the rocky slope. Instantly, the wolf could smell the tangy scent of blood in the air, and then he felt the sharpness of the man's body reacting to pain. The wolf's mouth watered anew and he stepped back to the edge of the cliff. The lanky man lay below, awkwardly splayed on his back amid the rocks. The light stick had tumbled further down the hill, as had the heavy black thunder-spitter.

The big man called out, now from near the armored beast. The lanky man moaned between gasps for air. He tried to bend to reach for his shin—which the wolf could smell as the source of the blood—

but was scarcely able to raise his own head. The big man ran toward his fallen friend, but then he too tripped on a rock and went flailing through the darkness before regaining his balance. He reached the light stick and used its beam to guide him to where the lanky man lay. There followed a long time during which the lanky man screamed in both anger and agony as the big man attempted to help him to stand. They were so engaged in this that neither of them noticed that the bound man was now also standing upright beyond the armored beast. Just as the big man was at last able to raise the still howling lanky man to a standing position, the now unbound man pulled open the flank of the armored beast, causing the buzzing sound to return.

The lanky man shouted something very short and harsh-sounding. Then the beast's buzzing stopped as its flank closed and it growled suddenly back to life causing its eye lights to blaze even brighter.

The lanky man pointed and screamed at the big man, who began using the beam of his light to search all around the rocks at their feet. The lanky man struck him in the head and raged louder than ever, repeating his short harsh word. The big man let go of the lanky man, who crumbled into a screaming pile, and ran off toward the armored beast. The wolf watched the big man's light beam darting along the ground as he tried to find a clear path through the rocks. It was too late, though. The unbound man had guided the armored beast to move backward and then to turn its round legs toward the dry lake bed beyond. It then leapt forward, bounding smoothly back in the direction of the human's usual territory—where their hard, black stretches of land extended from horizon to horizon. The big man ran after it, shouting. As the wolf had suspected earlier, he wasn't very fast at all. The big man continued to run after the armored beast long after the red lights of its tail and the dim yellow light of its still open rectum had vanished. Then the big man tripped once again, his light stick dropped and went out.

From his perch on the top of the mesa, the Mexican grey wolf threw back his head and released a long howl. An instant later, he felt glory at the mixture of pain and terror that exploded from lanky man among the rocks of the desert floor below. In the distance, he heard the return cries of his pack brothers and he bounded away toward the place where the slope of the mesa allowed for a controlled descent. There he would lead his brothers to their first kill of the night.

Seated on the edge of the cliff, his body cocked at a slightly acute angle, the old man remained, his expressionless, stone-like face staring into the cold desert night.

# The Ones that Aren't Crows

**[Beginning of Recorded Material]**

They all said it was a whale that we hit. Never mind only a few people on the boat claimed to have seen it. Never mind that no one ever found a carcass. It was just what we had to have hit. Survivors said it. State officials said it. Witnesses at the campground said it. That damn marine biologist with her migration charts said it. Hell, at the time, even I said it. And, of course, there was the media saying it. *The Seward Whale Strike Tragedy,* they called it. Twenty-five people dead. The worst accident in Alaska's tourism history since Will Rogers' plane went down in '35, they said. Oh, it was a tragedy, for sure. And hitting a whale in Resurrection Bay ain't exactly impossible. Depending on the time of year, the bay's full of them. But we got all sorts of regulations and restrictions to prevent strikes. Accidents do happen, but the only whale kills I'd ever heard of were from the bigger cruise ships, not smaller boats like I piloted.

I spent thirty years as a tour captain on those waters and saw everything that lived in them, from otters, to squid, to orcas. I've seen hundreds of whales. I know what whales look like. What I hit that day [...]

**[Coughing]**

[...] it was no whale.

**[Coughing]**

Excuse me.

I don't guess my saying that's going to come as a shock to you. I doubt your magazine would have sent you this far if you thought I was going to say "whale" when you got here. I know monsters and UFOs and weirdness is your bread and butter, but I thought I'd better say it up front. For the record and all. I'm about the last person you'll find who'll give you the real story. Probably the only one alive who knows it, too. But someone's got to set the record straight, so why not the guy they said caused the whole thing?

**[Coughing]**

Yeah, if there was anything everybody agreed on other than it being a whale that we hit, it was that it was my fault we hit it. They all said I was going too fast. Said I was drunk. For the record, though, I wasn't drunk. I said the same thing back then, and there was never any proof otherwise. Thing is, I'd had some problems of that nature in the past. I was still on probation with the company. So the Weasel's people made sure the alcohol got brought up. They were right about the speed, though. I was going 30 knots, which is 10 faster than I should have been by law. I admitted that much then and I still own up to it now. I shouldn't have been going that fast. But what I really shouldn't have done was listen to the Weasel.

**[Laughing]**

I been calling him "the Weasel" for eleven years, now, but you'd know him better as […]

**[Name redacted]**

His family made it clear what would happen to me if I soiled his name with any crazy accusations. Don't guess it really matters any more, since most of them are gone, too. I'll let you decide if you want to call him by his name or not. All your readers really have to know is that the Weasel was a bigwig official from Anchorage who'd pissed off a lot of people. Seems he made a bunch of promises to get himself reelected and then didn't keep a one of them. That's never happened before, right? […]

**[Laughing]**

**[Coughing]**

**[Coughing]**

[…] Sorry.

Like I said, a lot of people were gunning for the Weasel before the election and plenty more got in line afterward. Somehow, the folks who seemed the maddest were the Chugachs. I always thought that was strange, because the Weasel claimed to be part Salchaket, himself. I never knew exactly why the Chugachs were so angry with him. Something about sacred land or fishing rights, I want to say. Maybe both. What mattered was they'd figured out the Weasel was in Seward for some official ceremony at the SeaLife Center and they came to protest him. I know, 'cause I had to walk through them that morning on my way to the ship. I was nursing a headache and the noise they were making was [...]

**[Coughing]**

**[Coughing]**

Sorry. Damned stuff's [...] tightening its grip.

**[Labored breathing]**

I was on my usual Tuesday schedule that day, piloting the boat, the *Aunt Nancy*, on a four-hour sightseeing tour through the Kenai Fjords. The Nancy was actually sold out, but the company decided to let the Weasel on anyway. Said it would get us some publicity. Guess they weren't wrong on that count.

**[Laughs]**

Getting out on the tour was about the only way the Weasel could get away from the protestors. Whole bunch of them had followed him right down the dock and nearly up the ramp to the lower deck. Once he was safe on board, he seemed happy enough, even though he had to leave all his lackeys back on shore. I saw him wave at the protesters as we pulled away.

He didn't seem too enthusiastic about the tour. Gorgeous June day, cruising past some of the most beautiful scenery on the planet and the whole time that asshole just yakked into his fancy satellite phone. He didn't listen to the ranger's tour. He didn't eat the box lunch. He didn't press the flesh with his constituents. He just stood at the bow of the upper deck, right outside the wheelhouse's front window and yakked, while the deckhands brought him White Russians from the bar. I didn't really care what he did. I was told to keep him happy and if he left me alone in the process, that was all the better. But he didn't leave me alone.

Just after we'd seen the last glacier on the tour and had started back home, the Weasel got real interested in visiting the wheelhouse. He was all smiles, handshakes and vodka breath, at first. But pretty quick, he started hinting that he'd like to see how fast the boat could go. Wanted me to really open her up, he said—just for kicks. I tried to laugh it all off and quote regulations to him, but he was insistent. Said he had an appointment he had to keep. Made it sound like an emergency, even though it was probably just some gal.

I wish I could say he threatened me or even bribed me, but he didn't. In the end, I was just tired and my head hurt and I knew the sooner I got us back the sooner he'd be out of my hair. So I went faster. We weren't going top speed by any means, but the Weasel didn't know that.

We passed Caines Head, doing 30 knots. Probably pissed off the ranger, too, 'cause he had four minutes of chatter about the history of Fort McGilvray, all timed out to the geography. Soon enough we were in the home stretch, passing Lowell Point, within sight of town. I should have slowed down right then, but the sonar fishfinder was quiet and our path ahead was all clear.

Only, then it wasn't.

People say events happen in slow motion during accidents. I'd heard it, but had never experienced it until that moment.

I only glanced down at the gauges for a second, but when I looked back up there was a kayak in our path. I can still see it as clear in my mind as I did in that frozen moment. It was single-holed kayak, like the natives make, covered in spotted sea-lion skin. It floated stationary in the water, as though it had been there for minutes already. There was a man in it, wearing one of those native jackets they make out of seal guts, covered in sheets of red and black and turquoise beads. And he was wearing one of those wooden bird masks, like the kind they sell in native art shops, only his was old and worn. I can remember the chips in the paint of its red-lined black beak. Its eye holes were ringed with blue and black. And I saw the guy lift one of his arms and in his hand it looked like he was holding an egg. There was no way we could avoid him at that point, but I reached to cut my engines all the same. Just before he disappeared under the bow, though, I saw that man in the bird mask fling that egg into the water. Then he was gone and that's when the fishfinder started screaming.

It was a proximity alarm the likes of which I'd never heard before. I didn't even have time to look at the display when the ship jolted and our bow came out of the water. We had hit something, and it wasn't just a crazy fool in a mask, either. But nothing short some kind of a gigantic ramp made of rock could have sent a boat the size of the *Aunt Nancy* into the air like that. Not at only 30 knots.

**[Coughing]**

Time […] Time seemed to slow down again. I could see the Weasel framed in the port door of the wheelhouse. I could see individual ice cubes tumbling from his White Russian, chased by beads of Kahlua. I could hear the screams of the passengers on the viewing deck outside. Then the *Aunt Nancy* rolled to port and I was finally able to catch a glimpse of what we'd just struck.

[…]

It was a whale.

[…]

I know […] I told you before that it wasn't a whale. And it still wasn't. But that's what it looked like when I first saw it. An adult, blue whale—longer than the ship, flat head, grooves in the chin, the whole bit. And as the boat rolled in the air, looking down on that whale, all I could think of was how much hellfire the conservationist groups were about to rain on my head, assuming I lived through it. Then the upper deck plunged into the water and everything got dark.

I think I was knocked out there, for a while. When I came to, I was on the ceiling of the wheelhouse and I realized we were capsized. The lights were blinking on and off around me, the engine was screaming, and water was pouring in through the door. The cold woke me up quick. Even in June, Resurrection Bay is nothing but glacier runoff. The Weasel was there, too. He was flailing through the water, trying to climb out of it onto the slope of the ceiling that it hadn't yet reached.

Then the engine died and the lights went out. I could hear screams from the observation deck, which was also now above our heads. And then I could see forms thrashing in the dim light from the surface, outside the bow window. It was like staring into an aquarium filled with the bodies of passengers, strug […] strug […]

**[Lengthy coughing fit]**

[…] No. […] No, don't call the nurse. I'll […] I'll be all right in a minute.

**[Coughing]**

Don't […]

**[Sipping water]**

Where was I? […] The water. […] Water was still pouring in the wheelhouse door. I didn't know how long our pocket of air would last, but I knew if we didn't get out we were goners for sure. I could see the Weasel by the light from his satellite phone. I grabbed him by the arm and started pulling him toward the door. It was tough, though, because he kept fighting me. Then the boat shifted, again, throwing us back into the water. The *Aunt Nancy* had been floating almost exactly upside down, but it began to roll to stern as the lower deck filled with water. My view through the wheelhouse's front window rotated toward the surface of the bay. I could see people swimming on the surface. Others were motionless beneath the water. And beyond them, probably 200 feet away, was the shape of the whale. I thought it was dead, but then it turned and [...]

**[Long pause]**

Like I said, I've seen hundreds of whales. I know how they behave, how they move. This one didn't move like a whale should—or any animal, for that matter. One second, it was hundreds of feet away. And the next second, that whale was on top of us. I mean instantly, he was right there outside the window, his eye pressed up to the glass, looking right at us. That's when I saw that the whale's skin was wrong, too. It wasn't the usual gray-blue color of a blue whale. It was turquoise, and the eye itself was rimmed in black. And as the whale swam past the window, I could see the circles of red and black continuing down its body. Then its fluke passed the window, only it wasn't a fluke anymore. It was a wing, covered in black feathers.

**[Coughing]**

Bear with me. This is where it gets strange.

I never really saw the whale change—not exactly. I just sort of noticed that the whale wasn't a whale anymore, but a gigantic black bird. And, just like the whale, its feathers were painted, black and red and turquoise. It looked like something you'd find perched on top of a totem pole.

I watched the bird float there for what felt like a long time. The Weasel watched it too, but he was screaming. Then, just like the whale had, the bird lunged forward in an instant. It smashed its head through the wheelhouse's bow window. There it was, this impossible, gigantic thing, its black and red and turquoise body plugging the hole it had just made. I could smell its feathers, wet and old. The Weasel kept right on screaming until the bird's red-lined beak closed around his head. It stared at me for a second. Then, I think it… I think it winked. I'm not embarrassed to say I started screaming then, too, and kept on screaming until the bird wiggled its body out of the window, and Resurrection Bay crashed in on me.

**[Coughing]**

I […] I have no idea how I got to the surface or how I came to be in one of the rescue boats. Out of the 34 people on board the *Aunt Nancy*, only nine survived. Probably would have been fewer or none, if the Weasel's phone call to shore hadn't got the rescue crews moving. The papers said he was a hero who went down with the ship. I couldn't exactly tell them what really happened to him. I was in enough trouble. But you know all about that.

**[Coughing]**

What did I see that day? Well, it weren't no whale, that's for damn sure. What was it? Well, that's another name I don't like saying. You can't live in Alaska, though, without being exposed to more than a few of the native legends. They sell them to the tourists by the bagful and carve it into every stray scrap of wood, they can find. And the main character of all those myths and legends? It's a bird. A trickster and a shape-shifter, named after one of them black birds—the ones that aren't crows. They say he brought light to the world by stealing the sun and carrying it into the sky in his beak. And if he could carry the sun like that, I figure how much easier is it to carry away the life of a Weasel.

**[Coughing]**

So. Was it the ending you were hoping for?

Yeah. I thought you might have had a notion. But I doubt knowing the true story will do you any good.

**[Coughing]**

It's brought me nothing but grief and pain, but that'll end soon enough.

I wasn't kidding when I said I was the only one alive who knew the real story. The other eight survivors are gone already. So are a lot of other people who were there. The Weasel's lackeys. A couple of reporters [...] That damn marine biologist with her migration charts [...] All gone. Accidents, of course. Or [...]

**[Coughing]**

[…] or illness. […] They call it the Curse of the Whale-Strike Tragedy. […] I don't know […] about all the death. My only guess […]

**[Coughing]**

[…] my only guess is that it's […]

**[Coughing]**

[…] a warning […]

**[Coughing]**

[…] that it's dangerous to look into the face of a […]

**[Coughing]**

[…] of a […]

**[Coughing]**

**[Coughing]**

**[Coughing]**

**[Coughing]**

**[Coughing]**

**[End of Recorded Material]**

# The Wise Ones

Rain fell from the dawn sky, scattering what little light was able to reach the surface of the harbor. The rain seemed to ooze down upon the city, making those beneath it feel sad and more than a little bit afraid. It was the sort of rain that one could very well expect something dark and nasty to slither from—or, perhaps more horribly, to walk.

At this early hour, the only signs of any activity were from the fishermen, turning their boats seaward, and from a single light shining from the front picture window of a small building nestled among the bait shops and tourist traps of the harbor district. The building itself was an ancient structure composed of chipped, gray bricks that appeared to be held together by crumbling mortar and sheer will alone. A sign of cloudy brass hung above the front door of the building. It read simply, *Antiques*.

The light from the shop's picture window mingled with the rain on the boardwalk. Just inside the window, in a large, brown La-Z-Boy recliner sat an old woman drinking black coffee from a rustic-looking clay mug. Her long, thinning, silver hair was pulled back with a ribbon. Intense, brown eyes peered through the wire-framed relics which sat on her nose. On her lap rested a withered, wooden cane with a knobby, tarnished, silver grip. Beside her chair lay a stout dog. It was a muscular dog with black fur that blended into a reddish color on its underside. The dog's exact breed was uncertain—though the word *Rottweiler* seemed to stick in the minds of people when they saw it.

The old woman set her mug on the table beside her chair. It was another of the unique pieces found in her shop in that the table's body was that of a large mortar and pestle standing nearly three feet in height. The mortar itself was made of wood, banded in iron, and looked to be quite old. Its opening was covered by a notched glass top that allowed the long handle of the pestle to extend from within.

"This day is silent to me, Ursa," the old woman said with a frown. The dog's ears twitched at the sound of its name and it sat up, waiting for any further words it might know.

"On your guard," the old woman said. Ursa sniffed in reply, then got up and looked through the glass of the front door, staring into the dim beyond. The dog allowed herself a single, preemptive woof, but it was mostly formality. She could see nothing except the rain.

The woman lifted her bony, robed frame from the depths of the chair, straightening to a symphony of popping joints. Turning, she studied her chair for a short time before then adjusting it at an angle to face in the direction of the front door instead of toward the window itself. Next she crossed the area rug by the front door and dragged the free-standing coat tree from the right side of the door to the left, where it would be nearer to her chair. From among the array of coats there, she pulled a tall, yellow, hooded raincoat, and hung it again on a nearer hook. She found a pair of galoshes, as well, and placed them on the floor beneath the coat.

Lifting her coffee mug from its place on the mortar table, she started onto the center aisle when she saw the far edge of the area rug had been folded during the relocation of the coat tree. She put her mug back, then stooped to adjust the rug so that it once again covered the dark stain on the board beneath it. Retrieving her mug, the old woman said, “Come on then. Let’s see to your breakfast.”

They walked along the center aisle, among the tables and shelves, each filled with items more ancient than the last. She paused near the rear of the shop to consider the immense statue of a roughly sculpted clay man that stood there. It had a hatchet protruding from its face, splitting a word etched into its forehead. The old woman touched the handle of the hatchet, but then seemed to think better of it. She crossed the threshold of the door at the rear of the shop and turned left into the dimly-lit hallway beyond.

In the shop’s small kitchen, Ursa munched on dry kibble from a metal dish while the old woman, as was her custom, ate two pieces of toast, one with butter and jam and one with egg salad. Afterward, she refilled her coffee cup from the percolator on the stove and crossed the hallway to the door that opened into her bedroom.

The hallway held many doors—pairs of them across from one another, like the kitchen and the bedroom. Each door was made of unpainted wood with four identical, rectangular, inset panels, though their handles and doorknobs often differed. The kitchen, the bedroom and the door to the shop were among the few fixed points of geography the dog could rely upon and she rarely strayed far from them. There was another door her mistress visited nearly every day, one which Ursa had never ventured through herself. The air beyond it smelled of clean sheets, disinfectant, and breath. Its proximity to the other three doors was not always consistent, however. Occasionally the old woman ventured through other doors in the hallway. Ursa had accompanied her mistress on business within the rooms on only a handful of occasions. They were not among her favorite memories. She was usually content to nap in the sun in front of the picture window of the shop. With no sun this day, though, she remained in the kitchen, on the rug in front of the stove. She slept there, her dreams filled with images of toothsome creatures springing at her from behind closed doors.

An hour later, the dog was awakened with a start by an odd noise that seemed to come from the shop. It sounded like the noise of feet falling to the floor; first one pair, and then another.

Ursa crept from the kitchen into the hallway. Her mistress's door was closed. There was no sound from within it. There was a rotten, sulfurous smell from the direction of the shop door. It caused her fur to bristle. Moving to the door, she peeked around the corner. There, beyond the tables and shelves, standing just inside the front entrance of the shop, were two men. The tall man was smiling. The short one smelled of fear. Ursa pulled her lips back to reveal her own teeth, a low rumble of a growl already in her throat. The men did not move.

In the distance, Ursa heard the sound of her mistress's door creaking open, followed by her steps and the sound of a cane tip ticking against the floor. It seemed to take her mistress longer than usual to cover the distance from her bedroom door to the entrance of the shop. She was garbed in a long brown dress covered by a pale blue cardigan, her hair now pulled back neatly into a bun, held in place with a long silver pin. Her right hand held the grip of her cane; her left hand, her coffee mug.

The old woman stepped through the shop door, halting beside the statue with the axe. Ursa gave a gruff bark and followed close behind.

"The shop is not open for business," the old woman said with weary irritation. "I would have thought the locked door would have told you as much."

The taller of the two men took a step forward, continuing to smile. Ursa had never seen any of the films of the Hammer Films studio. She would not have known the actor Christopher Lee from his role as Dracula in a number of the films produced by that studio. If she had, though, she would have noted that he bore an unsettling resemblance to the taller man in the front of the shop. He wore a black suit beneath a tremendous leather coat with wide shoulders. The coat's surface appeared wet and scaly in the light. A single, blood rose rotted in his lapel and a wide-brimmed, black fedora rested above his ashen face. He removed the hat and bowed slightly.

"My mistake, dear lady," the man said in deep tones also borrowed from Christopher Lee. "I'm afraid I am unaccustomed to using doors." He replaced his hat, smiling all the while.

The shorter man—if you could call him a man—began to snicker. His appearance was remarkable—though Ursa did not know this, either—in that it was incredibly similar to that of actor Peter Lorre. Except for his gleaming red eyes and the fact that he reached a height of only three and a half feet, he was an exact replica of the late actor. He wore a tight, algae-green suit, which somehow seemed too small to fit his lumpy body. Atop his head was a black derby. He continued to laugh in a high pitched gurgle until he noticed Ursa's snarling approach, at which point he darted behind the tall man's legs, his Peter Lorre eyes bulging.

The old woman took a long sip from her mug and said, "Are you now?" Her expression, which had flashed briefly with anger moments before, now settled into something resembling an inflamed vexation. She leaned on her cane, moving awkwardly down the center aisle. When she was within a few feet of the men, she stopped.

"How may I help you?" she asked.

The tall man's grin widened. It was the kind of smile that takes a very long time to master.

"I take it that you are the owner of this particular shop?"

The old woman gave him the slightest of nods.

"Ah!" he said, his eyes brightening. "Then, unless I miss my guess, you, dear lady, would be the famous *Madam Z*?"

For a long moment the only sound that could be heard was the rain on the boardwalk outside. "I have been called by that name," the old woman said at last.

"Indeed," the tall man said. "Among many others." He seemed pleased. "Allow me to introduce myself," he said, bowing low. "I am called Bisley. And this," he said indicating the small man peering from behind his legs, "is my associate *Mr. Ramond*." The short man tipped his hat and flashed his red eyes briefly in her direction before returning them to the still snarling dog.

"What a true pleasure it is to finally meet you," Bisley said, beaming. He seemed jubilant nearly to the point of tears. "I've… You'll have to forgive me, dear lady. This is a momentous day for me. You see, I have been searching for you for… well, for what has felt like a very long time indeed. And now I am here and we are meeting at long last." He extended a gloved claw for the old woman to shake. She did not even look at it. After a moment he coolly withdrew it, closing his lips. He gestured to his surroundings, as if noticing them for the first time.

"This shop of yours, here… It is so very… quaint," he said, turning to stroll past the front window of the shop, beyond which the rain continue to beat against the boardwalk. "I can't say it is the sort of place in which I expected to find a person of your distinguished status. But then," he added, casting a sidelong glance at her, "I presume that was your intention."

If the old woman was at all troubled by him, Ursa could not detect it. If anything, her mistress seemed weary as she began moving slowly toward the front of the shop, her cane tip bumping against the rough wooden boards under the gaze of the tall man. She reached the mortar table beside her recliner and set her mug upon its glass top before turning back to her visitors.

"So," she began. "You and your syndicate have found me." Her tone contained not a hint of concern.

"You are familiar with us then?" he said. "What am I thinking? Of course you are. I should have expected no less." His smile remained in place for what seemed a very long time, with no response from the old woman. They simply stared into one another's eyes. Without looking away, the old woman brought her coffee mug back to her lips.

"Yes," she said. "I am aware of you and your so-called wise ones. While your kind has only returned to the shores of this plane recently, your stink has lingered long from previous incursions."

"No incursion, dear lady," Bisley said. "We come only when we are invited."

"Except for today," she said. "I recall issuing no invitations to your ilk for visitors at this hour."

Bisley's eyes narrowed, but he accepted this with a nod.

"You know, dear lady, you are an extremely enigmatic and controversial figure in the circles I travel," Bisley said. He turned to walk along the row of bookshelves that lined the far wall, Mr. Ramond close in tow. As he talked, Bisley's gloved fingers extended to trail over the spines of the books there, some of which had been out of print for well over two hundred years—a scant few of which had never been touched by a mechanical printing press at all. "I've heard so many stories… so many names…" he said. "Madam Z in some circles. Miss Zeddie, in others." He notched up his smile before saying, "Omega." There followed a long pause as he regarded her face for any reaction. Whatever he saw there must have pleased him, for his smile dropped not a mote. "To describe you as *legendary*," he continued, "does not even seem appropriate in the face of all that is said of you."

"Those who choose to believe rumors are apt to be disappointed," the old woman said.

"Rumors," Bisley said. "Second cousin to stories. Yes, I have heard quite a few of those as well. One cannot believe them all, of course. There are many that are contradictory. However, they do their part in adding to the… bigger picture." He stopped walking suddenly, noticing that the dust on his fingertips had grown thick enough to begin crumbling into small piles on the lip of the shelf. Mr. Ramond then walked into the back of his legs, causing the taller man to stumble. Bisley shot a vile glance behind him that made Mr. Ramond scurry back a few steps. Pulling a dark red handkerchief from a pocket, Bisley wiped away the dust from his gloves, before turning to flash his Christopher Lee smile at the old woman once again.

"Were you aware," he said, "that some *rumors* put your age at several thousand years?" He casually spun a yellowed globe in a dark wooden frame, allowing it to turn until bringing it to a halt with a finger pressed onto a continent which no longer exists. "I confess, I have not achieved that age myself, but it is an attractive thought."

He began his stroll anew. "There are, at the very least, reports of your appearance at numerous points in the history of this plane of existence alone. The larger debate, of course, is whether you truly are that old at all. There is even more debate, however, as to your actual appearance."

The old woman turned her back to him and moved to her chair, leaning hard on her cane as she lowered herself. Once she was settled, she lifted her mug again and took a sip.

"There are those—and, mind you, I have spoken to many, many souls—who have described you as a silken-haired lass with beauty beyond compare." He sucked on his bottom lip at this, regarding her with a skeptical and somewhat disappointed eye. "They actually said that. 'Beauty beyond compare,'" he added. "And these were not ancient old men who spoke of you. The tales they wove were of the recent past, or so they claimed."

The old woman drained the rest of her coffee and sighed. "I really should have brought the whole pot," she said, setting the mug back onto the mortar table.

Bisley looked annoyed momentarily, but then brightened. "That's a rather unique table," he said. "It reminds me of another rumor about you. That you are merely a witch who has survived the ages through spells and magicks. I find this to be one of the more boring explanations of you. However, some claim that you are actually the Baba Yaga, masked in a new identity." He licked his lips. "Your table would seem to stoke that flame of rumor. Am I to believe your shop has chicken legs beneath it, also?"

"Believe what you like, Mr. Bisley, but I am not Russian," she said.

At this, Bisley laughed. "Ah, Mr. Ramond. I knew I would like her."

Mr. Ramond began to giggle again.

"Dear lady, I do not believe you are the Baba Yaga, for the real Baba Yaga has been dead for over two hundred years."

"Closer to three," the old woman said. "If the rumors are to be believed, that is."

Bisley allowed his mouth to turn down ever-so-slightly. "That is the question of the hour." His eye lit upon the small likeness of a black panther, sculpted in coal, resting on a low shelf in front of him. He picked it up and examined it. "Some say you are an angel on assignment from the All Mighty himself. Some say just the opposite. Which rumor am I to believe?" He put the cat back, not bothering to fit its feet back into the four footprints in the dust. "Still others say you were once one of the Ascended Masters. You are said to have been demoted from their ranks for some infraction or other and now spend your remaining years as a mortal." He studied her, looking for reaction. "At the very least, you're known to have associated with others of the so-called descended. Kindred Spirit and his ilk." He turned to Mr. Ramond. "Wait. How did that one phrase it? Ah, yes. He said you used to 'hang with the big boys.' Yes, I think that's how he said it." Mr. Ramond gave off a giggle that held undertones of rattling fluids in his lungs. "The list of those who are alleged to be your allies and even former allies is actually quite impressive. Truly. I share a few enemies among your former friends. It makes us allies of a sort, no?"

The old woman's expression was not one of agreement.

"Then, of course, there is the list of your actual enemies, which is considerably longer," he said with some glee. "I did note that a number of your enemies are known to be woefully imprisoned beyond reach. A goodly number of others are, shall we say, missing?"

Bisley stopped by an open-faced cabinet filled with dust-covered bottles and glass colanders. Only a few of the bottles were labeled. He toyed with one that appeared to contain a small cloud.

"More than one of those I've interviewed has sworn to have been present at your birth into this world." He sighed. "When exactly that occurred no one can agree upon, of course. Perhaps more interestingly, though, a number have claimed to have been your lover." He allowed this to sit in the air between them, watching the old woman's expression closely before continuing. "They were liars—I could tell. Though I detected some truth in rumors of a lost lover from your past. One of the *big boys*, as it were." He set the bottle with the cloud back inside the cabinet before moving past the golem with the axe in its head and onto the center aisle.

"There's even a persistent rumor that you actually work as a carnival fortune teller one day out of every year." He chuckled, joined by Mr. Ramond's gurgling snicker, which now sounded like someone—perhaps Peter Lorre—being drowned. Bisley moved down the center aisle toward the old woman's chair, cocked at its angle toward the front door, Ursa at her feet. The dog growled as he came close, which prompted him to slow his pace.

"In all my inquiries, though, the astounding thing I have noticed is not the number of conflicting stories told regarding you, dear lady," he said. "What astounds me are the number of individuals I've met who, by all accounts, have had confrontations with you in the past… beings who should have stories about you of their own… but who, somehow," he said, "do not."

The old woman looked up at him, then lifted a hand and waggled it at the wrist in the universal sign for *get on with it.* "What business do you have with me, Mr. Bisley?" she said.

"My business," he said curtly, "is a proposition—one I am most certain you will accept… dear lady."

"I very much doubt that," she said.

Bisley chuckled. "At least hear me out. I have invested a considerable amount of my time and effort in locating you. I would hate to leave without making a formal proposal."

The old woman blinked at him slowly but remained silent. Bisley seemed to take this as an invitation.

"Rumors, dear lady, are in no short supply. I admit they can be delicious, but I am a man who appreciates a nice rare fact," he said. "I believe that you and I are very much alike. Our methods may seem different on the surface. At heart, though, we are simply information brokers. We deal in facts. We know a great deal about the workings of the planes of existence, as well as the various major players in the grand game." Bisley seemed to taste the words as he spoke them, relishing their flavor. "There has always been a market for people in our line of work—the ones who hold the big secrets of the universe. I like to think of myself as a consultant in *revenge maintenance.*"

Bisley began to pace up the aisle again, Mr. Ramond following nervously behind.

"There are, for instance, a plethora of individuals in the spectrum of planes and realities who, shall we say, *have it in* for other individuals. That spectrum of planes and realities, however, is filled with lots of places to hide." He shook a finger in the air, the folds of his great leather coat squeaking as he did. "This can make things very difficult indeed on the revenge-minded soul." He turned back, placing a hand upon his chest. "My revenge consultation services help ferret out such targets. I have made quite a name for myself in this regard. But, then, I expect you know that already," he said with a grin. "After all… *I* found *you.*"

The old woman removed her glasses and, retrieving a tissue from her sweater pocket, took her time cleaning them. "Yes," she said in a bored tone. "You found me. And how many others now know of my whereabouts because of it?"

Bisley's smile returned at an even higher curve. "The two of us, of course," he said gesturing to Mr. Ramond. "However, I have taken certain precautions that we are not the only ones. There is another soul who had many interesting things to say about you. He led me to your doorstep, as it were—though I confess you were not easy to find even with the basic geography he provided." Bisley took a moment to brush an errant cobweb from his sleeve. "I took the liberty of freeing him from his woeful imprisonment, as reward for his assistance. He is most eager to repay you for all you have done to him. Even in his weakened state, I doubt it will be long before he calls upon you."

Mr. Ramond gave off another of his gurgling laughs.

"He won't have as easy a time of it as I did. But then again, I am still for hire." Bisley tapped the side of his long nose. "Once I've been to a place, I can always find it again. No matter where that place might move." The tall man moved his hands to his side, in a kind of plaintive shrug. "Of course, I can also be persuaded to make certain he never finds you at all."

The old woman loudly blew her nose into the tissue from before. Bisley's smile wavered briefly at this. "What you're saying, Mr. Bisley, is that you wish me to join forces with you?"

Bisley smiled. “As perceptive as I expected,” he said. “Revenge, dear lady. It is a lucrative business. But it can also be slow and laborious work. My clients may have to wait a considerable amount of time as I do the legwork necessary to locate the intended target of their revenge. There is always the risk that too much time will pass, and their anger will cool. My services have, on occasion, been cancelled.” His smile vanished. “If there is anything I despise, it is effort wasted.”

“You should charge a fee,” the old woman said.

Bisley moved toward her again, stopping just on the other side of the faded area rug in front of the door. “While legends of your origin may differ, dear lady, there are a few things on which everyone who knows of you can agree. You are renowned for your ability to root out hidden information—even information long thought lost to the sands of time. And you have a tremendous knowledge base when it comes to the mystic hustle and bustle of the various planes of existence.”

“Is that why you felt it necessary to bring a null-imp?” the old woman said, with a nod in Mr. Ramond’s direction.

“Handy things, they are,” Bisley said, patting Mr. Ramond on the head. The short man’s high-pitched voice tittered to life again. He tipped his derby to her, causing Ursa to snarl. “I was, of course, advised that you do not appreciate unannounced visits. In fact, that is the third point on which all of my sources have agreed,” Bisley said. “I’m certain that Mr. Ramond’s presence will ultimately prove unnecessary. Still, I thought having someone along who could selectively turn off any mystical power sources might prevent any... unpleasantness, shall we say?" Bisley reached into the interior of his glistening, black coat and brought forth a dark red envelope.

"I hope you don't mind," he said, "but I have taken the liberty of drawing up a writ of retainment." He slid from the envelope a sheet of brittle papyrus on which generally unintelligible slashes had been marked in an odd coppery color. "This document explains, basically, that you would be held on retainer to me and would be entitled to..."

"I do not care."

Bisley looked up from the document. "I'm sorry?"

The old woman stood up from her chair, not bothering to support herself on her cane in the process. "I will not do business with you, nor any other of your kind," she said simply.

Bisley stared at the old woman with his deeply gray eyes, stolen from another man, his mouth a tight thin curve. After a brief moment, the lips opened partially to allow a chuckle to pass through. It began to grow. And as the laugh grew, so did his mouth, which expanded into a hideous, toothsome wall, his eyes dancing above it. Then the wall opened and his gale-force laughter burst from it. The unholy sound grew in intensity as the tall man's jaws became a spreading cavern, his features pushing aside to make room. Beneath the foul laughter was a grotesque whistling, like that of a sick animal's labored breath. Accompanying it was the gurgling titter of Mr. Ramond.

Ursa, who had begun snarling viciously at the tall man's first chuckle, now gave a low whine that was drowned out by the cacophony. She looked up at her mistress for assurance. The old woman stood firmly in place by the brown La-Z Boy recliner, her expression of dull anger never once faltering.

With one final, tremendous roar, Bisley ceased his laughter and all was silent except for the echoes of the sound from the infinite hallway. His grinning mouth returned to its previous size and he wiped a single green tear from the corner of one eye.

"My dear lady," he said in a soft voice, "you do not seem to understand your situation. The writ is a formality. There is no choice in the matter."

"There is always a choice," she said. Leaning her cane against the mortar table by her chair, she reached and took the long yellow raincoat from its place on the coat tree by the front door.

"Choice?" Bisley said after a moment. "I assure you that there is only one that is good for you." His ire seemed to grow with each passing second.

The old woman continued to bundle herself into the coat, closing its open front with peg and loop fasteners.

"Remember, dear lady, I hold your greatest secret—the secret you would be wise to keep from your considerable enemies at any cost." The sky rumbled forth as lightning struck nearby. "I know where you live."

The old woman scowled at him. Undaunted, he continued.

“There are beings in the universes who would give me my heart’s desire simply for the knowledge of the continent on which you reside. What more would they offer me to lead them to your front door?” he said. He tapped his nose once again. “How will you fare when the Shuddering Sadies come with their needles bared? What of the Cult of Mologox? The Weavers of Old?”

The old woman sighed, sat down on her recliner and began pulling galoshes onto her feet. Then, still stooped, she looked up at him and her face resolved itself into an expression bordering on pity.

“You’re all alike,” she said.

Bisley practically spat each word of his response. “Of what collective are you now speaking?”

“You and your syndicate and all of those who’ve come before you, of course,” she said. She gave him a scolding look. “Did you truly think you were the first one to make it this far, Mr. Bisley? The first to threaten me with exposure to my enemies?”

Bisley frowned. Behind him Mr. Ramond was feverishly wringing his hands.

“They’re always so very smart, when they come. Gloating about how they’ve finally found me… How I’m now bound to serve their every whim,” she said. She pulled the hood of the coat over her head, being careful of the silver pin in her hair. “They never quite think things through completely. If they ever did they wouldn’t make the same stupid mistakes every time.”

His grin twitched. “And just what mistakes might those be? What indeed?”

“Believing me to be powerless, for a start,” she said.

Bisley’s grin shot back to its previous strength. “You are powerless! You couldn’t conjure the energy to light a match with Mr. Ramond present!” Mr. Ramond cackled at this. “What are you going to do? Beat me with your cane?”

It was the old woman’s turn to laugh, which she did in a brief, loud burst. It was a sound Ursa was unaccustomed to hearing and it made her edgy.

“You truly thought you were the first to come here, didn’t you?” the old woman said.

“Enough games,” Bisley said with a glare. He took a ghastly, taloned pen from his pocket and shoved it and the ancient-looking paper in the old woman’s direction. “The writ, if you please.”

“Allow me to demonstrate the error of your ways, Mr. Bisley.” The old woman pulled the lever on the side of her chair, reclining it. She put her thin hands behind her head and lay back in the chair. “I can put a halt to your grand plans without moving from this chair.”

“You are beaten!” Bisley screamed, an undercurrent of fear in his voice.

“In fact,” she said, “I can defeat you using only three words.”

“Incantations won’t save you now!”

“Not an incantation,” the old woman said with a sly smile. “Merely a command.”

"And what would this command be?"

The old woman pulled her hood down over her face and said, *"Ursa... sic him."*

There was the briefest of pauses during which no sound was made. Then there came a snarl followed by the sound of dog claws scraping on wooden boards as Ursa leapt at Mr. Ramond. He uttered a porcine squeal and began flailing his arms. Ursa landed on him with a thud, sending his Peter Lorre body crashing to the surface of the area rug in front of the door. His derby went sailing into the air, landing somewhere among the shelves.

Bisley's formerly grinning Christopher Lee face lost its will to remain intact. His mouth fell open. He seemed to want to scream, but nothing came out. Mr. Ramond, on the other hand, gave off a high, gurgling wail that echoed from the walls. His jaw began to piston open and closed, modulating the cry. Then all noise from his throat was abruptly halted as Ursa's jaws clamped around it and she began to shake him violently. Mr. Ramond's smoldering red eyes bulged with fear and he began feebly clawing at the dog's fur with his pudgy hands, now stained black from his own blood. During the struggle, Mr. Ramond's form began to shift and change, giving off quick glimpses of something green and slug-like beyond the Peter Lore surface—something with piercing red eyes frozen in terror. Then, as his neck snapped, the illusory appearance vanished, revealing the imp's true form, blackness pouring from its neck.

"No!" Bisley howled. And he too began to change. His Christopher Lee form seemed to become hazy and indistinct as a shadowy darkness engulfed it. Within the darkness, Bisley's silhouette began to morph, until there seemed to be something large and vaguely cat-like within the darkness in his place. That was when Ursa began to shake Mr. Ramond's body fiercely, sending rivulets of blackness into the air. The gore landed on the area rug, and the nearby shelves, and fell into the darkness of Bisley's not entirely coalesced new form. Wherever the blood landed, the haziness solidified into a leather-like hide, while other areas remained hazy and in flux. Bisley screamed in pain and collapsed to the floor, his head mashing into more of Mr. Ramond's blood. His face instantly become a grotesque mixture of Christopher Lee and something feline.

There came a sound of wood scraping across glass. And then the old woman was standing over him, wearing her spattered raincoat and galoshes. She leaned past him and dipped something he couldn't quite see into the spreading puddle of Mr. Ramond's blood. Bisley tried to lash out at her, but didn't seem to be able to properly control the strangely-shaped limbs moving beneath the folds of his coat and he was only able to lunge out ineffectively with one arm. "The same stupid mistake," she said. "Null-imps don't work when they're dead."The old woman raised something above her head. It was the pestle from her chair-side table. She brought its thick, blood-coated end down on Bisley's one thrashing arm. He screamed as his elbow snapped. His arm ceased to flail.

"Their blood tends to linger on a while in its power, but it only affects what it touches," the old woman said, almost smiling. "Don't worry. We'll have plenty of time."

Ursa gave Mr. Ramond one final shake and dropped his body to the carpet. There was no hint of Peter Lorre about him. He looked, instead, like a slug, with two fat little arms and legs, melting away in a pool of salt.

The old woman threaded the pestle back through the notch of the table-top and didn't spill even one drop of blood on its surface. She removed her raincoat and galoshes, and retrieved her cane. She then turned to Ursa and cheerfully said, "Good girl. Now go to the kitchen. I'll be in with a whole can of ALPO, directly."

The dog licked its lips and bounded toward the infinite hallway. Then the old woman returned her attention to the business at hand.

"Now, Mr. Bisley, I think it's time I taught you a thing or two about power," she said, moving slowly toward him. "I have several points to make. When I am finished, though, I think that you will only be able to recall three of them."

The grip of her cane gleamed, as though reflecting a brilliant light.

"First, dear sir," she said, spitting the words. "Tell me your secrets."

Bisley's screams were barely audible over the din of the pouring rain outside.

# The King's Last Nacho

From his aisle seat, high in the empty nose-bleed section of the Mid-South Coliseum, a youthful-looking Elvis Presley smiled as he watched two men pretend to hurt one another in the ring far below. Jerry "The King" Lawler vs. Cedric Hinds: a contest that had been billed as the *Match of the Century!* Of course, most matches produced by this particular wrestling association were billed as being *of the century*—each one a perpetual ascent to the pinnacle of human achievement. And if you didn't like this one, you could come back for next week's pinnacle.

Elvis's famous smile widened, though whether this was due to his enjoyment of the match or of the nachos he was stuffing into his mouth was not readily apparent. He loved wrestling—adored it with something close to vigor—and it was one of the things he had missed the most during his *unfortunate retirement.* Elvis was especially a fan of Jerry "The King" Lawler. He'd been a big-name wrestler back in the '70s, and Elvis had been delighted to see he was still in the wrestling business in the late '90s. That man had been at this game longer than most fans could remember and he possessed a keen sense of the dramatic, which allowed him to play a crowd like a

Stradivarius. Admittedly, Jerry "The King's" Stradivarius had been knocked around a bit, and was occasionally out-of-tune, but it had been fine in its day and could still *eek* out a symphony when called upon.

Jerry "The King," in the purple trunks, leapt from the second turnbuckle of one of the ring's corners and fist-smashed his opponent, Cedric Hinds, in the green trunks. Hinds immediately fell to the mat, writhing in obvious pain, causing the audience to cheer. The referee stepped out of the corner of the ring to ensure that Hinds wasn't actually hurt. Hinds groggily tried to stand, displaying what in another venue could have been developed into a Cable Ace Award-winning acting ability. Hinds dropped back to his knees again, in obvious pain. Lawler paused a beat to allow the referee time to flee back to his corner, before offering his fallen opponent a hand to help him to his feet. Once both men were standing, Lawler turned the helping hand into an amiable hand-shake. And then Jerry "The King," still in possession of the hand, spun around and leaned forward, flipping Hinds over his shoulder and applying him with great suddenness to the mat. Upon viewing this outstanding display, no less than four spectators were moved to shed actual tears.

Wiping his own cheek with the sleeve of his shirt, Elvis chuckled. This was exactly what he had wanted to see, what he had missed for so long. He mused to himself that if he had devoted more time to watching wrestling and less time to other vices, things might have turned out differently for him. Instead all he had were hazy recollections of pill bottles, bullet-ridden television sets, stacks of fried peanut butter and banana sandwiches and lots of men in dark suits.

Out of that selection of recollections, the food was the most appealing. He had also missed junk food dearly. And as evidenced by the numerous wrappers, wads of grease-laden wax paper and plastic beer cups surrounding his seat, he was doing his part to regain his taste for it. He held his clear, plastic nacho-tray up for inspection. Next to the molded pit of cheese-like substance, a jalapeno cemented in place at the upper end of it, was one final nacho.

"You gonna eat that?" said a voice to his immediate right. Elvis nearly dropped the tray in shock. Two seats down there was a fat man wearing a stained khaki trench coat and a battered fedora. The left brim of the man's hat appeared to have been burned at some point in its no-doubt illustrious career. A deep five-o-clock shadow, and a smoldering cigar stub that jutted from the corner of his mouth, served to increase the air of slovenliness already stoked by the hat and coat. Elvis blinked at him.

"'scuse me?"

"That nacho," the fat man said, removing his cigar and cracking a smile. "Were you gonna eat it?"

"I was kinda aiming to," Elvis said, not certain if the man was joking. "Why? D'you want it?"

"Well, only if you weren't going to eat it."

Elvis looked down at the nacho and then back up. "Whyn't you just buy some for yourself?"

The fat man patted his coat front, as though feeling for a wallet which wasn't there, but didn't say anything.

"You don't have money?"

"Fresh out."

"How'd you get in here then?" Elvis said. "You some kinda reporter or somethin'?"

The fat man shook his head.

"I been sittin' here for forty-five minutes already," Elvis said. "Got a view of all the other closed-off sections up here. I didn't see you go through them and you sure weren't here when I sat down half hour ago. I'm askin' where you came from, mister?"

The fat man's smile faded. He puffed on what remained of his cigar before removing it from his mouth. "The truth?" he said, exhaling blue smoke.

Elvis nodded.

"M'aratos," he said.

"*Mara*-who?"

"*M'aratos*."

"S'that in Arkansas?"

"No," the fat man said in a flat tone of voice. "It's a star system."

Something in his stomach tightened and realization passed over the face of the King of Rock & Roll. "Oh," he said. "You work for *them* don't you?"

The fat man nodded.

"I was afraid of that," Elvis said. He popped the last nacho into his mouth, watching his new companion for any disappointment. He didn't see any.

The fat man cleared his throat and said, "This is usually the point when my face is supposed to go all shadowy and I say something like '*Men call me the Kindred Spirit.*'" His voice echoed mysteriously for a moment and his face did indeed appear more shadowy than before. "If you like, though, you can just call me *Kin*," he said, his face returning to his previous genial state. He offered his hand. Elvis looked at it but did not shake it.

"Wish I could say it was nice to meet you, Kin, but it ain't."

"Yeah, I can see how my being here might be a damper on your evening."

Elvis downed the rest of his beer in a single gulp, burped and stood up, sending empty chip packets cascading to the ground. "Well?" he said.

"Well what?" the fat man asked.

"Well, let's get it over with. Ya came here to take me back. So, take me, already."

The fat man looked puzzled. "All right. If you like," he said. "I didn't think you'd be in such a hurry, though."

"I ain't."

"Well then don't be!" the fat man said. "No reason to leave right away. We got all the time in the world."

Elvis looked at him with suspicion. He had expected that his former captors would eventually catch up with him, but this was not how he had imagined it happening.

"At least stay and finish the match," the fat man said. "Please. I insist."

After a moment, Elvis sat down again.

Below them, Cedric Hinds was wobbling unsteadily in the center of the ring while Jerry "The King" flew back and forth from rope to rope until he had achieved the needed velocity to launch himself at Hinds. His opponent was not caught off guard, though. As Lawler was about to pass again, Hinds held out an arm at neck-level, allowing Jerry "The King" to conveniently clothes-line himself on it. Lawler's chin caught on the arm, as planned, and his legs ran out from under him. The quick-thinking Hinds used the opportunity to drop his own body to the mat, slamming his arm into Jerry "The King's" neck as they fell. The crowd *Ooohed.*

"Oooh! That had to hurt," the fat man said, extinguishing his cigar stub on the concrete floor.

In the ring Hinds was the first to stand. He turned and waved to the crowd, most of whom were now booing loudly. After the allotted time for grandstanding, he turned and helped a smiling Jerry "The King" to his feet.

"I don't believe it!" the fat man said. "That guy's getting up! His neck must be as thick as it looks, takin' a hit like that."

Elvis stared at him for a while in cold contemptuous silence, but turned back to the ring after the fat man failed to notice. In the ring, Hinds began to attempt the same over-the-shoulder flip Lawler had used before, but this time Jerry "The King" was ready. Rather than allow himself to be flipped over Hinds's shoulder, he instead planted a leg firmly beside his opponent's spine and then rolled backward, allowing his own weight to drag Hinds up and over, launching him into the air and flipping him over in the process. Hinds crashed to the mat on hands and knees, collapsed and began writhing on the mat in another winning performance.

The fat man winced. "I take it you like this?"

"Yeah."

"Any particular reason?"

"Look, Kin," Elvis said, looking on the floor around him to see which of his other plastic beer cups might still have any beer in it. "I don't mean to be rude here, but I ain't havin' a real good day right now. I'm not much for talkin', if you don't mind."

"Say no more. Believe me, I understand completely." The fat man reached into his inner coat pocket and dug around for a moment before retrieving a cigar, which flamed into blue-smoking life, seemingly on its own. "I mean, why should you want to chew the rag with a guy who's about to take away your freedom?" The smoke from his cigar seemed to snake into a blue tendril around the fat man's head. It smelled sweet and earthy and not at all unpleasant. "If it helps, there's nothing personal in this," the fat man said. "I don't even directly work for the guys who're after you. I only took the job 'cause I'm sort of a fan of your work."

"You'll pardon me if I don't offer an autograph," Elvis said.

"No problem." The fat man was already busy searching in his coat pockets again. After removing a variety of items, including a souvenir spoon with a glowing jade dragon on the handle, a metal token with the word "Ryco" printed in relief on both sides, and a considerable amount of twine, he found what he had evidently been searching for: a square packet of candy in a bright red wrapper. The packaging featured a drawing of famed baseball player Reggie Jackson hitting a home run. The name *REGGIE!* was superimposed across it in large block letters, with a printed price of 25 cents in the upper right corner. The fat man set his cigar on the armrest of the seat next to him, then stuffed the previous items back into his pockets, tore open the wrapper and took a bite of the chocolate disc within. He smiled as he chewed and then offered it to Elvis, who had been watching the whole event. "You want a bite?"

"No." Elvis looked back at the ring for a few seconds before turning to face the fat man again. "What'd you just say about not workin' for the guys who're after me?"

"I don't work for the guys who're after you," the fat man said through a mouthful of chocolate, caramel and peanuts. He paused to swallow. "Not directly, at least. You wouldn't believe the amount of sub-contracting that goes on among the various cosmic agencies. It's a real paper trail. They have entire divisions to keep track of it all."

"Sounds efficient."

"Not really. See I'm subcontracted to an outfit that's subcontracted to the guys who were originally contracted to hunt you down. And those guys weren't the only ones on the job to start with."

"No?"

"Not by a long shot. Fortunately for you, most of the other bounty hunter types on your trail don't have a clue to share. Most. Unfortunately, some tend to be trigger happy in addition to being stupid. You don't want to deal with them." He retrieved his cigar and began puffing on it mightily. "In fact, I saw one of them before heading over here. He's staking out Graceland—like you were really gonna turn up there! Fabulous house, by the way. A lot smaller than I'd expected, but an impressive set-up all the same."

"Glad ya liked it."

"Hey, who wouldn't?" the fat man said. "Where was I, again?"

"The guys who are after me?"

"Oh yeah. Mindless turds, the whole bunch of 'em! Couldn't find ass at a thong competition. I mean, the moron at Graceland was actually sitting in a tree, like you were going to walk right up to the front door and he could grab you while you were looking for your keys. He may as well have been camped out in a lawn chair, with his gun in one hand and his thumb up his butt with the other."

Elvis couldn't help but laugh.

"I was shocked he made it to Memphis in the first place," the fat man said, the diffuse smoke from his cigar coalescing into a blue rhombus. "Those guys usually ignore the obvious places to look. Me, I figured you were probably here in Memphis because it was *too* obvious."

"I did go back to Graceland once," Elvis said in a soft voice. He stared out over the crowd in that distant way that used to boil hatred in the fathers of teenage daughters from coast to coast.

"You did? When?"

"'Bout a year after I got back to earth," Elvis said. "I kept a low profile for a long time, figuring I'd get snatched if I poked my head up or tried to see family or friends. Didn't figure anybody would believe it was really me anyway. Then some culty fan-club popped up saying they'd figured up the day of my glorious return—like I was the Second Coming, or something." He laughed. "I couldn't believe folks thought I was still alive, but they'd been saying it for years, it seems. This culty group said I had planned it all from the start—fakin' my death, waitin' around for decades until I was ready to make my big comeback, on exactly the day they predicted. Never did figure out how they arrived at that date. Something to with my birthday multiplied by my so-called death day, divided by the number of letters in my name, or something." Elvis shook his head. "I figured, who was I to argue with modern science? If I was supposed to come back on that day then I wasn't gonna be the one to disappoint 'em."

"You went?"

"I went."

The fat man waited, a look of anticipation hanging on his face. "And?"

"Not much to tell. None of 'em paid me any mind," Elvis said.

"That's human nature, for you," the fat man said. "They might've *said* they thought you were coming, but deep down they didn't really believe it."

"Probably didn't help that there were forty-nine *me*-impersonators running around, either."

The fat man laughed until he began a coughing fit that lasted for some time. When he had recovered, he said, "What possesses people to do the whole impersonator thing?"

"I dunno. Seem like nice enough folks. Hell, most of them looked better in the jumpsuits than I ever did."

"That reminds me," the fat man said, gesturing toward Elvis's trim form. "Whoever designed the new you must've been a real pro!"

Elvis looked down at himself. "Nice job, ain't it? It's my third one."

"Third?"

There was a pause as Elvis cleared his throat. "Yeah," he said. "I kind of bloated up the first two. Then they gave me this one. Probably the only good thing to come out of my *unfortunate retirement.* It can process junk food like it was broccoli and never gain a pound."

"What's it do to broccoli?"

"Don't know. I don't eat that shit."

In the ring, Cedric Hinds briefly gained the upper hand by climbing atop the third rope and hurling himself in the direction of Jerry "The King." He connected, but only just barely. The blow knocked Lawler to the mat and fueled his anger.

"Can I ask you something?" the fat man said. "If you're such a wrestling fan, how come you never made a wrestling picture?"

It was a good question, Elvis thought. He had seen hundreds of local matches, back in the '70s, and even more on TV. The live matches were his favorite, though. Each one of them had been completely individual in execution and yet each had followed the same basic script. The well-known, or *big-name* wrestler would, with varying degrees of style and grace, pummel unmercifully the unknown or no-name wrestler. The big-name wrestler would, naturally, emerge victorious at the end, only to have his title threatened by yet another fearsome, nearly anonymous warrior the following week. Once the big-name wrestler had several such victories under his belt, he would be pitted against another big-name wrestler for the championship match—*Of the Century!*—the winner of which would be given a title belt and bragging rights for at least a month. They might even be given a televised match against another big-name wrestler. That's where the politics really began.

The fact that the list of big-name wrestlers who won frequently matched the list of wrestlers whose ticket sales were highest was by no means a coincidence. Sure, one of the no-name wrestlers would occasionally graduate into name status, but such changes in the drama tended to happen with great subtlety, and usually over a period of years. And if a formerly popular wrestler's ticket sales began to flag, why then it was time for a widely-publicized retirement complete with a widely-publicized, victorious final match. Six months down the line, following an intensive weight-training program and the deletion of the usual hanging gut, the "retired" wrestler would announce his return in a hurricane of publicity, delighting and amazing fans throughout the region. The whole thing was about as genuine as… well, professional wrestling.

"Can't say I rightly know," Elvis replied.

"Seems like it would have been a natural step in your film career, considering all the other pictures you made."

"I did make a lot of pictures."

The fat man gave him a big grin. "I've seen every one," he said around his cigar.

"Really?"

"Yes, sir. I know a little theater that runs 'em every Tuesday. As luck would have it, I'm always free on Tuesdays. Seen 'em all—some three or four times."

There followed the customary span of silence that always accompanies such a bold statement.

"Even *Clambake*?"

"Even *Clambake*."

Elvis raised his eyebrows. "Yeah. Sorry 'bout that one. It was kind of the beginning of the end."

"It's an acquired taste," the fat man said. "But a wrestling picture… Now that at least would have made sense, is all I'm saying."

Elvis blinked. "I guess. Closest I ever came to wrestling was that boxing picture—the remake of that old Bogart/Robinson film."

"*Kid Galahad*? Great movie! You were way better in that role than Wayne Morris was in the original."

"*Thank'y'ver'much*," Elvis said. "Wish I coulda worked with Bette Davis, like Wayne did, but it was a pretty good picture." He became pensive for a moment. "I probably came too late to the party for a wrestling picture. I used to watch it in the service, but I didn't get to really love it until '68 or so. By then, I was more or less out of the picture business. We were plannin' a comeback to acting for '78, but that didn't happen, for obvious reasons."

"I'm sure it would have been a classic," the fat man said.

"Maybe."

At that moment, no one in the audience screamed at the referee. The referee turned around to see who it wasn't. Jerry "The King" seized the opportunity and lifted Cedric Hinds, by one arm and the back of his bright green trunks, then deposited him over the ropes and out of the ring. Hinds landed awkwardly on the side of his leg and then smacked his head against the padded floor. A cheer arose from the crowd. The sound seemed to confuse the referee and he squinted into the audience, oblivious to the illegalities behind him. On the floor, Hinds was not writhing as much as he had before. Jerry "The King" nervously peered down at him for a few moments before starting his triumphant strut around the ring. It was supposed to be a short-lived, pre-victory, mini-victory. In fifteen seconds, Hinds was scheduled to rise up from the floor with a shouted defamatory statement that would prompt Jerry "The King" to climb out of the ring himself for a hearty round of chair-fighting. After twenty-five seconds, though, Hinds had still not arisen. Jerry "The King" continued his strut, the audience cheering him on. Finally, after nearly ten more seconds, Hinds stirred, painfully found his feet, and coughed a family-friendly vulgarity into a microphone that happened to be taped to the corner pole nearest him.

"I realize you might not be too thrilled about this particular subject but I gotta ask," the fat man said. "Why'd you do it? Your retirement, I mean?"

Elvis shook his head. "It's actually a pretty stupid reason. You sure you really wanna know?"

"I do. It's been buggin' me for a long time."

"It'll ruin the mystique."

"Oh, please. I know the full name of the guy who faked the Shroud of Turin. Ain't nothing gonna surprise me."

"You're sure, you're sure?"

"I'm sure. Tell."

"All right. Don't say I didn't warn you." Elvis paused for a long moment. "Toilet paper," he said.

The fat man's expression did not change except for his eyes, which slowly shuttered closed. "I was wrong," he said after a while.

"Told ya," Elvis said. "See I wasn't doin' too good in '77. In fact, things were pretty much goin' to shit by then. One day these lil' sumbitches showed up at my door askin' me if I wanted to leave and go away with them for an exclusive concert contract. They didn't say *where* I'd be going, at first, but I figured it wasn't good from the way they looked."

"Like what?"

Elvis suppressed a shudder of anger. "They looked exactly like my Mama and my dead twin, Jesse. Only they sounded like a couple'a Atlantic City mobsters and they were dressed in black leather."

"Yep," the fat man said. "I know the type."

"I told 'em to go to hell. At least, at first. And they went," Elvis said. "Next day, though, some different clowns showed up. Only these were dressed up like Krishnas or something, wearing white robes and carryin' palm leaves. They said I should stay right where I was and not go with nobody, no matter what I was offered. I told them to go to hell too. Then I told the boys to watch out for any more of them. Didn't help. Different folks showed up every few days, most of 'em askin' me to leave with 'em. Some of 'em were making pretty big offers, promising all sorts of things. Most looked pretty crazy, too. I got the hell out of town, went to Vegas. But they started showin' up at the penthouse—bumpin' on the glass in their big black space-ships or pretendin' to be bell-hops. They stopped coming round so much when I took to shootin' at 'em."

"Good for you," said the fat man, his cigar smoke coiling around his hat band.

"So one day, I'm back at Graceland, restin' on the toilet, and I come to find out I'm outta Charmin. There weren't none in any of the cabinets and I wasn't too keen on trompin' through the house for any, on account of I wasn't feelin' too solid that day. The boys were out by the pool and I'd given the staff the day off. I was beginnin' to think I was gonna have to use a towel when outta the linen closet walks the sumbitch that looked like Mama, holdin' a fresh, cushiony, apple-scented roll of T.P. She said, 'You want it, you gotta sign with me.' And I'm sorry to say, I took it."

The fat man shook his head in disgust.

"I wish I could say I was hypnotized by that roll of toilet paper," Elvis said. "I can't though. By then I was just sick of it all; the booze, the pills… all of it. No, I took that roll of my own free will. Next thing I know, my old body's lyin' on the bathroom floor and my mind's in a brand new one. All the haze my life had become was gone and I was gettin' whisked across the stars in a space-ship."

Elvis reached for a large popcorn bucket on the floor by his seat and began picking through the kernels at the bottom. "It wasn't so bad out there at first. I was singing again and for some of the most appreciative audiences since that first *Sullivan* show—even if they were strange-lookin'. After a while, though, it became routine. I got bored and had to get out," Elvis said. "Escapin' from 'em wasn't all that difficult, once I put my mind to it. It was gettin' back to Earth that was the challenge."

"You pick it up as you go," the fat man said.

"Once I got back I figured I'd better hole up somewhere in case they were lookin' for me. Took me a year to figure out it wasn't doing me any good. I was just imprisoning myself," Elvis said. "I'd been readin' the tabloids, an' all—keepin' up with whoever Lisa Marie was marrying that week. From what I gathered, though, people had been claiming I was still alive for years. Nobody paid much mind to it, though. Made me think no one would pay much mind now that I *was* actually back. I was even thinkin' of startin' a new career. Maybe claiming to be one of my own long-lost illegitimate sons, or something." Elvis sighed. "Looks like it's back to the keepers with me now."

The fat man extinguished his cigar on the floor and stuffed the butt into a coat pocket. "I hate to have to be the one to do it, too. Only reason I took this assignment is 'cause I'm such a fan. I just wish there was any other way."

"You could let me go," Elvis said.

"Nope. As much as I'd like to, I can't do that. I'm contractually obligated to find you and bring you in. No substitutions allowed."

"You could tell 'em I overpowered you," Elvis offered.

"Heh, no," the fat man said. "You might have an eighth degree blackbelt in Karate and I might look like a fat tub of shit, but you just put that out of your mind. Nobody important would believe I didn't wipe the floor with you. It's a reputation thing."

"Hm. Well, I guess that leaves us where we were, then," Elvis said.

"True. But when you think about it, that's actually a fairly interesting place to be."

"How's that?"

"Bureaucracy."

"What about it?"

"Are you kidding? It's everywhere. All around us. From governments, to corporations, to cosmic organizations, not unlike the one I'm currently contracted to."

"Uh huh."

"You're not following me are you?"

"Nope."

The fat man reached into the inner recesses of his coat and rummaged around for nearly a minute before pulling his hand free. With the hand came a small avalanche of material including what appeared to be some parking tickets, several full packets of airline peanuts, a map of Haiti, and a wallet-sized photo of Soupy Sales. Clutched within his grip, however, was a small white card marked with what appeared to be thin, gray, horizontal stripes. The fat man rummaged in his pocket again and brought forth a colossal Boy Scout magnifying glass, which he held above the stripes.

"Here we are," he said. "According to my contract, if the detained—that's you—is able to best the detainer—that's me—then the contract for capture will become null and void. Then you get to go free."

"'*Best you*'? Like a fight? You said I wouldn't have a chance."

The fat man read over some of the lower-most, proportionally smaller, sentences. "Says the conditions of the *besting* can take place either following the detained's third successful escape from the detainer or by the detained's defeating the detainer in a fair and pre-determined contest."

"Well, that's a pretty stupid clause. I just have to escape again?"

"No. You have to escape me three times."

"Okay."

The fat man chuckled. "Not gonna happen, though. For one thing, I am *not* one of the aforementioned *mindless turds*. You may have escaped those guys fairly easily, but I am something else altogether. When I am contracted to go and get a person, I go and I get that person and they do not escape me even once, let alone three times. If they *were* to escape—which they never ever do—I would go and I would get them again and I would arrange it so that they didn't escape anymore."

"Another reputation thing?"

"Exactly."

"So then I have to defeat you in a contest?"

"That's about the size of it."

Elvis sighed. “What’s the contest?”

“That’s the fun part. We get to choose.”

Elvis’s brow furrowed. Then it brightened suddenly and he smiled. “I think I see where you’re goin’ with this. You wanna have a singin’ contest, don’t you?”

“Good God, no, man. You’d slaughter me! No, this has to be a fair contest. The card says so.”

“Well, what then?”

The fat man thought for a moment. “Obviously it can’t be singing or guitar playing or anything musical because you’d have an unfair advantage. It also stands that it can’t be a knowledge-based contest. I don’t mean to be insulting, but the index on just the useless information in my head would be more than enough to boggle yours.”

“Fine. I get the picture. If we can’t do music or egghead then what’s left? Flippin’ coins?”

The fat man smirked. “You wouldn’t say that if you knew what a mean sense of irony God really has.”

“I thought you said you saw *Clambake*?”

“Point taken.”

They pondered this in silence, enveloped by the noise of the spectators below. Something stirred. The fat man looked toward the ring. “We could wrestle,” he said.

“What? You and me?”

“No. Not you and me physically.”

“Then what?”

"Well..." the fat man paused. "Wagering is fair, right?"

"I suppose."

"And we've got a perfectly good wrestling match on our hands here."

"Are you serious? You wanna bet on the match?"

"Yeah! I bet on one guy, you bet on the other guy, we wait and see what happens. If the guy you choose wins you go free."

Elvis was dumbfounded. "Kin, I gotta tell you something about this..." He stopped and looked at his shoes for a moment. They were blue suede. You couldn't get good blue suede out in the cosmos. He looked up. "I gotta tell you... I think this sounds like a plan."

"Well, all right, then!" the fat man beamed.

"I get first pick, right?"

The reply was a sour laugh. "Nothing doing. You're a fan of wrestling. For all I know you got odds and statistics on both of these guys."

"But..."

"Me? I don't know either of these guys from Adam. I have to rely on my wits and observational skills to make the choice. That way it's fair." If the fat man saw the expression of doubt and bewilderment flow into Elvis's face he didn't let on. Instead, the man pulled his fedora low on his brow and turned studious attention fully to the ring.

"Hm," the fat man said after half a minute. "They both seem pretty evenly matched to me. Both of them have thrown the other guy out of the ring, so they're both strong. They've also been at this for a good while now, so they've got pretty good stamina. Now the one guy is a lot older than the other, so I could choose young guy and hope he out-lasts the older one."

Elvis's ears perked up at this.

"Then again, age equals experience and skill, and those usually win out over youth," the fat man said. "What are these guys' names again?"

"Cedric Hinds."

"And?"

Elvis sighed. "And Jerry 'Th—uh, Jerry Lawler."

"Huh."

The heart of the king of rock & roll sank. Then, in the ring, a seemingly dazed Cedric Hinds took advantage of a two-Mississippi pause, during which Jerry "The King" had turned his back to wave at the crowd, and reached out to wrap an arm around Lawler's head from behind, deftly executing an inverted facelock before dropping his weight to the mat, seemingly wrenching his opponent's head in the process.

"Er… Maybe not," the fat man said. "Lawler's lookin' kind of tired."

"Look, if you don't hurry up they'll be done and we'll be back where we started," Elvis said.

"I'm sure they got other matches coming up."

Jerry "The King" writhed in the ring, struggling to get his legs beneath him and avoid Hinds's attempts to get one of his arms trapped in a leg scissor.

"Seems to me that the choice can actually be narrowed down to one single issue," the fat man said.

"Yeah?"

"Do I choose green trunks or purple ones?"

Elvis's mouth began to drop open but he caught himself. Here it was. His ultimate fate determined by whether or not this heathen to professional wrestling chose the purple or the green. If it was green then the choice is Cedric Hinds, the no-name wrestler destined to lose, thus ensuring freedom. But if the choice was purple then the trunks belong to Jerry "The King" and freedom would be a thing of the past. Everyone—except, apparently, Kindred Spirit—knew that Jerry "The King" never loses to no-names. This was maddening.

*Dear God in Heaven,* Elvis prayed silently, *if there's any way you could intervene on my behalf I would greatly appreciate it. After all, I did record a darn fine Christmas album. Amen.*

"Green," the fat man said. "I choose the guy in the green trunks. The old guy's looking winded."

Elvis curled his lip into his world-famous smirk, folded his arms and sat back in his seat. "May the best wrestler win," he said.

Then a horrible thought struck him: what if—what IF—this match was Jerry "The King" Lawler's "retirement" match for the year? What if this was the match designed to allow Lawler a few months off while elevating Cedric Hinds into name-wrestler status? A victory over Jerry "The King" would be just the thing. Hinds could affix whatever nick-name he wanted onto his own name and bide his time winning matches against his former no-name brethren until it was time for the inevitable re-match with Jerry "The King." Elvis Presley's face fell and he sat back up and watched with anxious eyes. His expression turned to pure worry when, moments later, Cedric Hinds managed to secure Jerry "The King's" right arm in a leg scissor, immobilizing it. He then wrapped both hands around Lawler's face, locking his fingers across the man's forehead and pulling back with seemingly all his might—a move Elvis recognized as a *crossface*. "The King" was pinned. Members of the audience began to scream and boo and throw their beer cups toward the ring. Cries of foul and damnation were shouted as their hero lay writhing on the mat within Hinds's grip before their very eyes.

"Ah hah!" the fat man exclaimed. "Green it is! I knew there was some reason I liked that boy!"

The referee, who was somehow now paying attention, started the final fateful count.

*Three…*

Elvis could see it clearly in his mind's eye. It was the beginning of his countdown to incarceration. In mere moments he would be on his way back to the hellish existence he'd known before. Three shows a night, six nights a week, with nary a jar of peanut butter within six hundred billion miles.

*Two...*

Fate had been toying with him. This was his penance for all those pills... all the girls... the cheating on his marriage... all those thirty-pound bejeweled jumpsuits... *Clambake.* He was done for.

The count came to a sudden halt with a turn of events in the ring. Jerry "The King," despite the tremendous pressure being exerted on his neck by Hinds's grip, was able to maneuver his unpinned left arm from beneath his own body and—seemingly calling upon the strength of Hercules himself—shot it out on the mat beside him, using it as a fulcrum to pull both his own weight and, with a subtle assist from Hinds, seemingly his opponent's as well. Pressing with his knees and his free hand, he managed to roll to the right, pulling Hinds beneath him and, with a force of willpower and muscle, at last break free of the crossface. Hinds fell back dazed to the mat and lay there gasping for air. With the last of his strength, Hinds rolled to one side and reached out toward the corner where his manager stood, silently calling to him for help. His manager, a part-time theology professor from Chicago, took the Messianic symbolism to its full extent by choosing that moment to turn his back on Cedric Hinds. Then Jerry "The King" Lawler, clad in the purple trunks, planted a foot onto the mat and slowly and triumphantly rose to a standing position. Many members of the crowd broke into uncontrollable fits of cheering, which grew louder as Lawler climbed the ropes of the nearest corner of the ring until he stood atop the turnbuckles on either side of the ring post. In the ensuing chaos and crowd noise, no one took notice that Hinds's writhing on the mat had maneuvered him into a prime position to become the recipient of an acrobatic move from the top rope. Jerry "The King," ever the master of timing, allowed the tension build as he stood, surveying the coliseum, arms raised.

"Oh, this don't look good," the fat man said.

When they could stand it no more, he launched himself into the air, arms outstretched, falling almost parallel to the surface of the mat. At the last second, he cocked his right hand back in a fist and slammed it and his body weight into Cedric Hinds's chest.

The crowd exploded to their feet with cheering. Elvis leapt up with a whoop and joined his voice with theirs as Jerry "The King" pinned Hinds's limp form to the mat as the ref went through the count. When he hit one, the crowd lost their minds.

Elvis turned to look at the fat man. In that moment, it occurred to him that the idea of wrestling by proxy might—*might*—have been a joke all along. It was certainly absurd enough to have been. He watched the fat man's expression for any hint of this, and waited for the other blue suede shoe to drop. The fat man, meanwhile, was again digging in his interior coat pocket for something. With some effort he freed a lit cigar, but this caused another avalanche of trinkets and paper to spill onto the floor well, landing among Elvis's food wrappers.

"I've really gotta get around to cleanin' that out one day," the fat man said. He stooped to gather up his belongings and stuffed them back into his pockets. He took a long drag on his cigar and then said, "You won. You're free to go."

Elvis eyed him. "Just like that?"

"Yeah, yeah. You won fair and square, according to the fine print," the fat man said. "You're someone else's problem now."

They sat there for a few seconds, as the spectators in the lower seats began to file out toward the concession stands. There were only precious minutes before the next match began and they had to restock their snacks and beer.

"Guess I aughta say, thank you," Elvis said.

"Nah! No reason to thank me. Just promise you'll stay away from shitheels in trees."

"I'll keep an eye out for 'em."

"Make sure you do. Even mindless turds get lucky sometimes." The fat man stepped past Elvis and into the aisle, his trail of fragrant cigar smoke slithering behind to catch up. "It was great to meet you, Mr. Presley," he said, offering his hand. "I hope you find a way to get back into the music industry. Or, better yet, the pictures."

"I doubt that'll happen," Elvis said.

The fat man smirked. "Ah, you never know. Picture studios are always looking for someone to play a young *you* in a biopic. You'd be a natural."

"Yeah?"

"Sure," the fat man said with a grin. "Now, you would need to be able to sing, though."

Elvis laughed and shook the hand of the man called Kindred Spirit. He then watched as the fat man moved down the concrete steps of the empty nose-bleed section, trailing blue smoke. The smoke was really billowing, until Elvis could barely see the man's movement through the vapor. Then, the smoke dissipated and Kindred Spirit was gone.

For a long while Elvis simply stood in place, breathing in the aroma of spilled beer, with a distant hint of ring sweat. Then he decided he'd had enough wrestling for one day. He started to gather up his trash to go, but quickly noticed a thick, blue-and-white card lying on the floor in front of the fat man's seat. There were seven odd-shaped holes punched in the printed squares along its top edge and just below the holes was the logo of the wrestling association and the words *Season Ticket Holder*. Below those words, in smaller letters, were the dates of the past seven wrestling matches. And below that, in red ink, was the name of the ticket-holder. It read: *Ken Dredd.*

Elvis's mouth opened and closed. Then he read it again and a great big smile broke across his face. He looked around, as if the fat man might be lurking nearby to catch his reaction, but he didn't see him. Then, with a start, Elvis smelled the earthy smell of the fat man's cigar smoke and noticed blue vapor floating away from the surface of the card. The punch-holes had vanished and the red-inked *Ken Dredd* had been replaced with the name *L. Vess Priestly.*

"Thanks, Kin," Elvis said. He heard no response.

On his way out of the coliseum, the once and future King of Rock & Roll stopped at the concession stand and ordered a fresh tray of nachos.

# Puppet Legacy

Until Uncle Turley farted, the loudest sound heard in the house that day had been the clatter of pots and pans in Mamaw's kitchen as lunch was prepared. The outburst caught everyone's attention, amplified as it was by the vinyl upholstery of the recliner into which Turley had settled for his afternoon nap. The fart startled Aunt Della's dog, Fancy, set Amos to snickering, and caused Mamaw, who was nearly deaf, to look up, aghast, from her own chair.

"Turley!" Aunt Della scolded, whacking her husband across the legs with an issue of *Good Housekeeping*. "Keep your gasses to yourself! We have company."

Jarred from his slumber, Turley laughed and began to say something before Aunt Della rolled her magazine into a makeshift club which she brandished at him. "And if you say, '*My compliments to the chef*' you'll get one across the mouth!" she said. Turley chortled again, joined by Amos, but offered no further comment.

On Mamaw's floral-print sofa, Aaron leaned close to Stephanie and whispered, "Welcome to the family."

"You know, technically, I won't be a member of your family for three more months," Stephanie whispered back. "*That*," she added, nodding toward Turley, "might have been a deal-breaker."

"Oh, please," Aaron said. "If that's the worst thing we hear out of Uncle Turley this weekend, we can count ourselves lucky."

Aaron and Stephanie's impending nuptials had been the focus of earlier lunchtime meal chatter. With Aaron still in Tupelo and Stephanie in North Carolina, Aunt Della had been careful to make a big deal about how costly an interstate move would be for them, and how Stephanie might be best off selling most of her possessions beforehand. Aaron didn't mention that he would actually be the one making the move, and he was proud that Stephanie was able to keep quiet on that angle as well. He'd asked her to give him time to break the news in his own way, as he wasn't sure how Mamaw would take hearing that her grandson would be moving out of convenient visiting range. Aaron's visits were infrequent enough, and Tupelo was barely a three-hour drive away. It was a situation that had once prompted her to say, "Once your grandkids get grown, they just throw you to the wolves."

"Well, on that note," Aunt Della said, rising from her seat and offering her hand to Stephanie, "let me show you where *you'll* be sleeping." As Della had informed them during lunch—with a good deal more joy than Aaron appreciated—Stephanie would be sleeping in the back bedroom of the house, while Aaron would be sharing the middle bedroom with Amos. Aaron had assumed the two of them would be separated, and had told Stephanie this before they'd left Tupelo that morning. However, Amos was an annoying addition he'd not counted on. Aaron wanted to ask why his cousin couldn't simply sleep at Della and Turley's house, next door, but he knew that the real purpose for placing Amos in proximity was to guard against any nighttime bed-hopping by the happy couple. And Amos, a sour lump of a soul with a mop of red hair, was perfect for the job of guardian because his sleep apnea kept him on the edge of consciousness throughout the night. It, unfortunately, kept anyone sharing a room with him on the verge of madness as well.

Aaron wanted to find it insulting that his relatives thought so little of his self-control that they would impose such unpleasant inconveniences as Amos upon him, but he had to admit that they had a point. He probably would have snuck in to Stephanie's room, if only for a smooch. Or three. He couldn't help it, though. Victims of a long-distance romance, he and Stephanie had synchronized their vacations in order to see one another for a whole week. In just a few days, she would have to return to North Carolina. Every second counted. The only reason he had brought her to Mamaw's for a visit at all was because he wanted to introduce her to his crazy family in *advance* of their wedding. It only seemed fair.

While Della took Stephanie for the guided tour of the back bedroom, Aaron headed to the car to get their bags. Despite their sleeping arrangements, he was really looking forward to the day. He wanted Stephanie's first visit to Mamaw's farm to be special. He wanted her to experience this place where he had spent so much of his youth and to love it as much as he did. He wanted to show her the hayloft where he and his sister, Elaine, used to make tunnels through the bales—at least until Mamaw pointed out the possibility of snakes nesting in them; he wanted to take her down to the pond, and sit there beneath the pines; he wanted to show her the old cypress stump, which Aaron, as a four-year-old, had believed to be a sinister cat-like creature called a Hocco; and he wanted to sit with her on the porch swing, telling her all about the many summer nights he had spent there with his Papaw. Looking at the dilapidated old swing in the daylight, its coat of red paint worn away by backsides and weather, Aaron could still envision Papaw sitting in it, his right hand wrapped around a support chain, his foot lazily rocking the swing back and forth, as he told stories.

Papaw's stories were never the typical grandfatherly yarns one might expect of walking to school uphill in the snow, or buying milk for a nickel. Instead, they were more often about his years spent in the Civilian Conservation Corps, building roads across Wayne County and beyond, in the 1930s. Other nights Papaw had reflected to his later years spent working for the U.S. Forest service, stationed as a spotter in fire-towers throughout the county—including times when he had seen tornados tear across the countryside from a vantage point 400 feet in the air. Or, when Papaw was feeling especially festive and Mamaw wasn't within earshot, he had been known to tell of his adventures running moonshine with his brother Wilkin.

The tale Aaron remembered best was of the time they smuggled 'shine in from Alabama in the back of Papaw's truck by cleverly storing jars of it inside the truck's spare tire. They had stayed the night with a couple Wilkin knew, who had a two-year-old toddler.

They'd hauled the spare tire indoors to the kitchen for safe-keeping, but its contents proved unsafe from their own hands. Everyone had a pull or two from one of the jars within the tire and they were soon quite warm and happy, late into the night.

"We got woke up the next morning by the lady of the house screaming from the kitchen like it was a snake," Papaw had told him. "We ran in to see what was wrong and there, in the middle of the kitchen floor, is their kid, cockeyed drunk." Papaw had laughed long at this and it took Aaron a while to decipher that the child had drunk from the jar they'd left open the night before. "That was the drunkest baby I ever seen," Papaw said. "Just kept bumping his head into the chairs until he finally fell over. We didn't have time to laugh, though, 'cause the Missus came after us with a rolling pin and we had to snatch up our tire and skedaddle. Barely made it back to the car with our brains."

After laughing at this for what seemed twenty minutes, 12-year-old Aaron had said, "You sure did get in a lot of trouble, when you were young, Papaw."

At this, Papaw had just smiled wryly and said, "I ain't told you nothing. Ain't told you nothing."

Aaron went into the house with the luggage. Stephanie was again seated on the floral-print sofa. When she saw him, she pursed her lips together, as she always did when trying not to laugh. She held out a small object, a puppet with a blue cloth body, its wooden head carved into the likeness of a young boy. Aaron closed his eyes and groaned.

"Where did you find that thing?" he said.

"On the bed in the back room," Stephanie said. From the dining room, Aunt Della snorted with guilty laughter.

"What is it?" Stephanie asked.

"A puppet."

"I can see *that*," Stephanie said. "Why does it look like a little version of you?"

Aaron walked over and took the puppet from her. It did indeed resemble a much younger version of him. Its head had pink skin with rosy cheeks and carved blondish brown hair, the paint of which had been chipped over the years, revealing the wood beneath. Its eyes, though, had remained intact and were still almost the same shade of blue as his own. Its body was made of blue and white striped cloth that ran from its neck down to where its knees would have been, if it had had knees to begin with. Two sleeves extended straight out from the shoulders with dingy-pink cloth hands at each end.

"My great-aunt Regina made this for me when I was six," Aaron said.

"It's incredible," Stephanie said, taking the puppet from him again. "I've seen your school pictures and the likeness is perfect. It's got your little frowny face and everything. It's too cute!"

"Turn it upside down," Della said, walking over to them.

"No, she doesn't need to turn—" Aaron began, but it was too late. Stephanie had already turned the puppet upside down and pulled its gown inside out to reveal another puppet head beneath. The new head was almost identical to the first but for the presence of a tiny cloth Santa Claus hat glued to its head and a smile carved into its face. The gown had been double layered and the underside of it was made of the same red cloth as the hat, with tiny green buttons in a row up the front, a black cloth strip for a belt and the gluey remnants of cotton ball fuzz that had once served as trimming along the skirt edge and at the cuffs.

"Get it?" Della said. She took the puppet and flipped it over to the striped-blue side. "I *don't* believe in Santa Claus." She flipped it back to red. "I *do* believe in Santa Claus."

"Very clever," Stephanie said. "I take it someone was having a crisis of faith?"

"Something like that," Aaron said. "But, this thing got me believing again, for at least another year."

"I was just telling her how I'd had to clean out Regina's house, after she died, and it was just full of all the little crafts she used to make. I had to throw a lot of it out, but I kept the puppets she made of the family."

Amos mumbled something from the little brown chair by the wood stove, where he was flipping through an old copy of *Ladies' Home Journal.* There was never much to read at Mamaw's except for the Bible or women's magazines.

"Aunt Regina always put her best into the family puppets," Della said. "They're based on the old plantation flip dolls from around the Civil War."

"I'm not familiar with those," Stephanie said.

Turley cackled. "One side's white. The other side's a darkie!"

Della gave him a sharp look, but Aaron saw the corners of her mouth fighting to turn up. Turley continued to laugh at his own joke, affording Aaron the chance to lean close to Stephanie and intone through his teeth, "What did I tell you?"

The casual racism of his more southern relatives was one of the major drawbacks of introducing them to anyone. It was something Aaron's father, who had himself married into the family, had given Aaron strict caution against over the years. He had explained to Aaron long ago that Turley and even Papaw were of a different era with different attitudes. It didn't make them bad people, necessarily; just wrong. Turley was especially problematic, as he seemed to take pleasure in lobbing out slurs in otherwise polite company, almost as if he were testing to see who else might share his outlook.

Della raised her voice to be heard over Turley's racket. "Regina's puppets are all just the one color. Well, mostly," she said. "But they do tell little stories and jokes that she made up. There's a bunch more in the closet, back in your bedroom. The whole family's in there."

Amos grumbled again.

"Shall we go meet the rest of the family?" Aaron asked in a cautious tone.

Stephanie looked at him with a curious smile that didn't quite extend to her eyes. "Um… okay," she said.

As they left the living room, Turley called after them. "Don't let 'em tell you that's one of me in there. Cause it ain't!"

The back bedroom closet was indeed full of miniature family members, all arranged on a four-tiered set of thin wooden shelves, which used to hold spare linens. Even knowing what he would see before he opened the door, Aaron still found it unsettling to have that many sets of eyes fall on him at once.

"That's… kind of creepy," Stephanie said. After several seconds of staring in silent wonder, she added, "Do you know all these people?"

"No," Aaron said. "I've met a few, but most of them are old relatives long gone."

Stephanie picked up the puppet of a smiling blond girl holding an orange cloth carrot. "I recognize your sister," she said.

Aaron smiled. "That's not Elaine. That's my mother." He pointed over to the antique ladies' dressing table in the corner where there was a black-and-white portrait of the same small blond girl, smiling sweetly from within a tarnished metal frame.

"Oh, my God! The likeness is amazing!" Stephanie said. "What's with the carrot?"

"No idea. Regina always used her puppets to tell a story or emphasize a character trait, but I never heard what the carrot meant."

Stephanie returned Aaron's mother to the shelf and considered the rest of them.

"Is this your papaw?" she said, pointing to a smiling bald man.

"No, that's Uncle Wilkin, Papaw's brother," Aaron said. He glanced over the shelves. "No, it doesn't look like Papaw and Mamaw are even here."

"They're gone?"

"Missing in action," Aaron said. "There were some puppets that we weren't allowed to touch as kids, and Mamaw and Papaw were two of them."

"Why?"

"They were fragile, I guess," Aaron said. "Their puppets were some of the oldest Regina had made. They were kept on top of the big curio shelf in the living room, but were hidden for good after the grandkids got big enough to try and climb up to get them."

"Let me guess," Stephanie said, "you were the one to make the climb?"

"No, that was my cousin Gary Jr. He broke his arm and knocked out his front teeth when the whole shelf came down on him."

"What did they look like?"

"Like Mamaw and Papaw—only young. They were about the age they were in those portraits in the middle bedroom."

"Oh, they were young," Stephanie said. Then she paused. "I thought Turley said he didn't have a puppet?"

"Yeah, Turley says a lot of things," Aaron replied. He picked up a fat-faced, smirking puppet from the top shelf. The puppet's gown was made of denim and cut to look like overalls. One of its cheeks bulged with a plug of tobacco. He handed it to her.

"Of course it's him. It looks exactly like him. A little younger, maybe, but that's him."

"Turley doesn't think so. And he has pretty good reason to doubt it," Aaron said. "His puppet pre-dates him."

"What?"

"Aunt Regina made this puppet in 1952—fifteen years before Della and Turley even met."

"You're kidding," Stephanie said.

"I kid you not."

"But that's impossible. How can it be Turley if she made it fifteen years before? Unless Aunt Regina was a bit…"

"Na NA Na na, Na NA Na na," Aaron said, imitating the theme music to *The Twilight Zone.* That was the closest he could come to describing Great Aunt Regina's gift. She had been many things in life—generous, sweet-tempered and always ready to help anyone in need—but words like *psychic*, or *clairvoyant* just didn't seem to fit. Still, she had definitely known things that she otherwise shouldn't. Or couldn't.

"Your whole family is Na NA Na na," Stephanie said. She turned over the Turleyesque puppet, inverting its denim skirt to reveal the other side.

"It's… it's exactly the same," Stephanie said. She flipped it back and forth several times to compare, but from the tobacco bulge to the wild smirk that made it look slightly crazed, the puppet was indeed the exactly the same. "What does that mean?"

"My dad thinks it means that Turley is just Turley—never more or less than a big, ol', tobacco spittin' goober."

"That's sort of a mean interpretation."

"But is it wrong?" Aaron said with a grin.

"Mm," Stephanie said. "What was Aunt Regina's explanation?"

"She never gave us one. If anyone brought the subject up, she would just laugh. So we stopped bringing it up."

"That's… um, odd. But I kind of like her style," Stephanie said. "Oh, look—she made your dad too!"

"That's him."

"He looks so young. A lot like you do now, actually."

"She made that one when I was five, shortly after my dad had a dream that a monster killed him in this very room."

Stephanie leaned against the edge of the brown, metal bed-frame. "Are you trying to get out of this whole marriage thing?" she said. "Cause creepy psychic aunts and spooky monsters aren't helping your case."

"Hey, I survived your family," Aaron said with a grin. "You should at least know a little about mine."

Stephanie looked doubtful but flipped over the likeness of her future father-in-law all the same. Underneath, was not a second version of him at all. Instead, the skirting was armless and made of black cloth, extending down from a black, nearly featureless head. There was no real neck to speak of, causing the head to blend directly into the body. It looked something like a silhouette or a shadow, though one with yellow eyes and very tall ears.

"What is this? Batman?" Stephanie said. "Your dad is Batman?"

"It's not Batman," Aaron said. "It's the Hocco."

"The Hocco?"

"Yeah. The monster dad dreamed about. Only, *I* thought it was real."

"Oh, here we go."

"No, really. It's a cute story," Aaron said. "See, when I was about four my dad tried to teach me the concept of echoes by clapping his hands down near the edge of the woods. Only there was this creepy old cypress stump out there that I thought was the creature that made the…"

There was a sudden sharp cry that sang out, "The Hoccoooo makes the echoooo!" Aaron and Stephanie turned, startled to see Amos, his body practically wedged in the narrow doorway. He snapped open the lid of a Zippo lighter using only one hand, flashing them a satisfied grin. Aaron was instantly irritated. Not only had Amos spoiled the story, but he'd got the inflection wrong.

"I love that story," Amos said. "You should also tell her the one about when you tried to sleep-walk out the front door at 3 a.m."

"What do you want, Amos?"

"Oh, just checkin' in," Amos said with a knowing smile. "Momma wanted me to make sure you two were finding everything *okay*, back here."

Aaron started to respond that before Amos's untimely interruption, he had been on the verge of cramming his tongue down Stephanie's throat and then having his way with her. Before he could say it, though, Stephanie herself interrupted.

"I don't see a puppet for you in here, Amos."

Amos's lighter fell to the floor, bumping softly on the yellow utility carpet.

"Oh, that's riiiight," Aaron said, mimicking his cousin's sing-song inflection from before. "Amos doesn't have a puppet. Not anymore."

"Why not?" Stephanie asked.

*Because Aunt Regina could never find enough cloth to make even a miniature version of Amos's fat ass,* Aaron instantly thought. It was an old joke his cousin Gary Jr. had once said. And it would have made the perfect comeback in that moment—but Aaron decided to be nice, not only for Stephanie's sake, but also because it wasn't true. Amos did have a puppet. Aaron had seen it. He'd been given it a year after Aaron and Gary Jr. received theirs.

Amos picked up his lighter. "Momma prob'ly threw it out. Or put it on the burn pile."

"Why would she do something like that?" Stephanie asked.

Amos shrugged.

"Was it ugly, or something?"

Amos was silent for a long time. "I guess to her it was," he said.

Aaron tried to remember what Amos's puppet had looked like. From what little he could recall, it had simply been a likeness of Amos in all his grinning, red-haired, apple-cheeked, roly-polyness. Everyone had liked that well enough, but Aaron had only seen a glimpse of the flipside of the puppet. From what he recalled, though, the puppet had looked similar to the first side, only with Amos made up like a clown and wearing some sort of lumpy costume made of red velvet. The puppet had a curly red clown wig that looked to have been made with dyed fake fur. Instead of white greasepaint, its face was bare except for red lips and blue shading around the eyes. Aaron had always wondered if Aunt Della had a fear of clowns, because she'd quickly tucked it away into a grocery sack, along with everyone's wrapping paper, which she saved.

When Aaron looked up from his thoughts he found Amos staring back at him. There was something in his cousin's expression that told him they were both thinking of very similar topics.

"You told her, didn't you?" Amos said.

"What?" Aaron said, "Told her what?"

Amos didn't say, but Aaron thought he must have meant Gary's joke.

"Amos, I didn't say anything about—" Aaron began but then stopped. His cousin's face had changed. No longer was it entirely angry. Instead, the faintest of smiles had crept to his lips, pushing his fat freckly cheeks up.

"My puppet wasn't the only one they thought was ugly," he said calmly. "You should show her those others, out in the smokehouse." Amos's smile widened for a moment. "Yeah. Go show her the ghost," he said. He flipped open his Zippo once again, pulled a pack of cigarettes from his shirt pocket and headed toward the front door.

"What was that about?" Stephanie said in a low voice.

"I don't know. He's an asshole," Aaron said. "Maybe he found some other puppets out there, or something." Even as he said it, Aaron felt a knot of anticipation form in his stomach. It seemed somehow familiar, like something felt a long time ago, when he was barely old enough to read.

"Want to go see?"

"Sure."

They returned to the front room of the house to find Turley napping again, now joined by Mamaw in her chair. From the sound of it, Della was in the house's sole bathroom, just off the dining room. Aaron held up a finger to his lips and led Stephanie past Turley and the bathroom door, then into the kitchen where he lifted a thick ring of keys from a nail by the open utility room door. He held her hand, pulling her into the utility hall, pausing only to pick up a red plastic flashlight from the shelf of Mamaw's old pie safe, before leading on past the deep freeze and washer and dryer to the back door.

"Why are we sneaking?" Stephanie whispered.

"Old habit," Aaron whispered back. "You try growing up with a tattletale little sister and a mamaw given to sweet gum switches and see how much it hurts every time you bring a frog in the house." Aaron unlatched the back door. It only creaked a little as they stepped through onto the concrete back porch.

"There she is," Aaron said, pointing a short distance to the smokehouse. It was a stout, tin-roofed building that Papaw had constructed using homemade cement blocks, some of which bore etchings and handprints made by Aaron's mother and Aunt Della.

"That's where your papaw smoked meat?" Stephanie said.

"Never knew him to. Refrigeration put an end to that," Aaron said. "Papaw just used it to store tools and pesticides and his supply of snuff—you know, smokeless tobacco."

"I'm from North Carolina. I know what snuff is."

"Right."

As Aaron suspected, the smokehouse was still secured with a padlock. Fortunately, it was a Masterlock and there were only three Masterlock keys on the thick ring, so he wouldn't have to try all twenty-five.

"I don't know why you're bothering to sneak. Do you really think anyone still cares if you see a couple of old puppets?"

"Guess it depends who they're of. Could be Mamaw's puppet—in which case, yeah." He tried the first key. It didn't work.

"What's the big deal?"

"Are you kidding? She can't abide seeing pictures of herself. Why would she want a 3D representation hanging around?" He tried the second key. It didn't work.

"But you said her puppet was young—like her portrait."

Aaron shrugged. "Maybe the flipside looks as old as she does now. Ooooweeeeooooo!"

Stephanie gave him a look. "No respect for your elders," she said.

"You're spoiling all the fun," he said. He tried the third key. The padlock snapped open. "Bingo!" He lifted the lock out of the ring and pulled the latch plate open. "Prepare yourself," he said.

"Why?"

Aaron spun the wooden block above the latch, which held the smokehouse's door in place, allowing it to fall open. The interior of the smokehouse was a thick network of cob-webs and pre-cob-webs stretching between the rafters that held up the tin roof, as well as among the brimming shelves that lined both sides of the narrow aisle. It smelled like dust and tobacco, with a hint of decay. The shelves held old cardboard pesticide boxes, snuff glasses, snuff tins, tools, tarnished flatware, and layers of red dirt from the road, blown in under the door. The walkway between was relatively uncluttered, but for a few glass jugs, metal pump sprayers and two wooden crates filled with empty one-liter Frostie Root Beer deposit bottles. Beyond the end of the shelves, in the space where meat had once been hung to cure, was now a darkened sea of nondescript spider and possibly snake-infested bygone junk, most of which was piled into cardboard boxes. While no actual snakes could be seen, Aaron could dimly make out the shape of a two-quart pickle jar that was indeed filled with rubber snakes, which Papaw had used as scarecrows in his blueberry bushes. He would have to warn Stephanie about that. What he could not see from outside the smokehouse, however, were any puppets.

"Mind the cobs," Aaron told her, pressing the on button of his flashlight.

"Nope. You're on your own for this one," Stephanie said. "Let me know how it goes."

"Chicken," Aaron scolded. However, he wasn't feeling particularly hardy about venturing into such a spidery place himself. He picked up the handle of a broken hoe and used it to swipe away some of the webbing and webbing-residents before carefully stepping into the smokehouse.

As Aaron shone his light into some of the brittle cardboard boxes that seemed big enough to hold a couple of puppets he silently prayed that the puppets weren't in one of the boxes at the bottom of this packrat collection. He doubted that they were, if only because he couldn't imagine Amos putting in the kind of work necessary to find them there in the first place. Amos would have had to stumble on them by accident, probably while looking for hidden jars of Papaw's stash of moonshine.

"Any luck?" Stephanie called after he'd been at it for nearly four minutes.

"Lots of dirt dauber nests and things with legs," Aaron said. "Puppets, not so many."

There was a metal fruitcake container he recognized from a very early Christmas in his life. Its contents rattled in a very non-puppety sort of way, so he decided not to risk exposure to the ancient horror of whatever that unwanted fruitcake had become. An old milk churn seemed a likely hiding place, but it only contained the skeleton of a mouse and more red dirt from the road.

Just as Aaron was about to risk certain death from black widow fangs by lifting up the edge of what looked like an old push mower, he spied something familiar above eye-level. Hanging from a rafter on a hooked piece of thick wire was a green suitcase with a faded purple and black tropical print. It was very small and would have only seemed properly to scale for a four-year-old child, which was how old Aaron had been when his dad had first given it to him. He hadn't set eyes on this bag for at least 15 years. One edge of the bag's green plastic handle had torn away from its fabric surface, causing the whole thing to hang from the metal hook in a very precarious manner.

Aaron lifted the bag from the hook and set it on its side atop the surface of a half-broken wooden barrel. He didn't call out to Stephanie—he wouldn't until he knew for sure—but his gut told him that he'd found what he was looking for. Carefully, he unzipped the bag. After waiting the customary amount of time for anything within to escape on its own, he lifted the lid. Inside there was a moldy, inexpertly folded yellow towel. Most of it was wadded at what would have been the bottom of the bag, as it hung from the wire. From beneath one corner of it, Aaron saw a tiny, pink hand. The hand was not made of cloth, but carved from wood, its index finger pointing forward seemingly in his own direction. The sleeve of the arm had come loose from the hand, revealing a thick, braided wire that disappeared beneath the edge of the towel. He gently lifted the fabric of the towel and found himself staring down into the carved face of his great aunt Regina.

The sight came as a shock to him for two reasons: first, because he had never even known she had a puppet in the first place; and second, because her puppet had been partially burned. Almost half the red cloth that made up the puppet's body was singed away, and part of one of its heads had been blackened. But then either the fire had been put out or went out on its own, because the rest was intact, save for the soot. The top face, the one with the pointing hand, looked angry—downright furious. He had only seen Regina that angry once in his life, which was the time she'd caught him aiming his pellet gun at her dog, Sport. Aunt Regina had beaten Aaron with a yard stick from her house all the way back to Papaw's front porch. The look on the face, coupled with the pointed finger made Aaron feel chastised. He set it down.

"Anything?" Stephanie called.

"Just a second."

He reached for the towel, feeling it to see if it held any more surprises. A hard lump in one corner of the case told him there was at least one more. He pulled the towel toward him, unfurling its folds until at last it came away revealing the face of his papaw.

Just as he had recalled, Papaw's puppet looked exactly like the portrait photograph of him as a young man in his early 20s. The carved face was a perfect likeness of him, smiling handsomely, his dark hair carved as if combed back on his head, the crinkles around his eyes just starting to form—a testament to Regina's skill. His cloth puppet body was made of a dark fabric, cut to look like the suit he had been wearing in the portrait. A yellow shirt and blue tie peeked through behind the lapels in a triangle near its neck.

Grinning, Aaron reached down and picked up Papaw's likeness. He was about to turn and carry it out for Stephanie to see, but then stopped. His gaze had fallen upon the lower edge of the puppet's body, where the inner-lining of its flipside was just visible through a gap made by the bulk of the puppet's other head. The lining Aaron saw was white linen, as if made from a bedsheet. And licking out from beneath the edge of the fabric was a flattened cone of white, tapering to a point.

He flipped the puppet over and turned its dark blue skirt inside out.

Aaron froze.

*"Go show her the ghost,"* Amos had said. And Aaron now knew both exactly what his cousin had meant and why this puppet had been hidden away for all these years. Aaron recognized the blue-suited young man as his papaw. The little thing he now held in his hands, clad in its white-sheet robes and pointed hood, bore no resemblance to

the man he had known. Yet, horribly, Aaron somehow knew in that instant that it truly did.

Behind him, he heard Stephanie's voice distantly, but he couldn't make out her words. Instead, all he could hear was his own voice from fifteen years before, saying, *"You sure did get in a lot of trouble, when you were young, Papaw."*

*"I ain't told you nothing,"* Papaw had said. *"Ain't told you nothing."*

# Limited Edition

For a man who had once stood two feet from the angel of death itself, C. Phillips Hovelan, antiquities appraiser from the Hovelan Gallery of Chicago, was having difficulty believing the way his day was turning out.

The woman across from him started on her third pass at trying to convince him that the brown and crinkly document on the table between them was an actual copy of the Declaration of Independence. He had heard her story twice already and knew it well; how she had recently seen a television news program about a lady who had found just such a copy hidden within the frame of a painting, deep in an attic; how that copy had sold at auction for $8.1 million; how she herself had ventured into her grandmother's attic with the intent to find such a copy herself; how, after four minutes of searching, she had indeed discovered one hidden between a sheet of cardboard and the print held within a frame; and how she had now journeyed up from Myrtle Beach to attend this taping of *Antiques Roadshow* today. Her barely unspoken hope was that its sale would provide enough liquid cash for her to while away the remaining half of her life in opulent splendor. Hovelan had already attempted to dash this hope by twice informing her that this particular piece of paper was almost nearly worthless. The dashing had not been successful. Hope, as Hovelan had personally observed during his twenty-four years as an appraiser, was far too strong a force to be destroyed by the application of mere facts.

It was Hovelan's personal policy never to be rude to delusional guests at his table. His usual method for accomplishing this was to sic his producer, Toni, on them. Toni, however, was standing with her back to him, about twenty feet away, and no amount of his mentally willing her to turn around had produced any effect.

Now the woman was beginning her story anew, as though he had missed a crucial element that would prove her paper to be authentic, and Hovelan decided a break in policy was required. He released a bite of his inner cheek from between his teeth, adopted his most erudite tone, looked down his beak-like nose at her, and began to speak.

"Madam, I must again inform you that you are incorrect. Your document, as I have already noted twice, is in no way an original copy of the Declaration of Independence," he said, lifting it by a corner with a pair of rubber-tipped tongs. He shook it in her face. "This…obviously press-spawned knock-off, in point of fact, looks nothing at all like the hand-written original document from 1776." He released the tongs, allowing it to flutter to the green-velvet upholstered tabletop. "No, madam, yours is merely a mass-market reproduction printed for the Centennial Celebration of 1876. There were thousands printed exactly like this one. I don't know why people of your grandmother's generation felt it necessary to squirrel them away in the backs of paintings, but it is of no consequence that they did."

"But the one on the TV…" the woman began.

"The one you saw on '*the TV'* was probably one of the original copies distributed to the thirteen original colonies," Hovelan began. "It was quite a find for its owner. Yours, as I believe I have now amply expressed, is not. The value of this piece is not in the seven-figure range, but is closer to the twenty-to-twenty-five cent range." He allowed a pause for this to sink in. "However, if you would care to use your paper to the fullest extent of its value, might I suggest that you fold it four ways and use it to wipe—"

Before he could reach the graphic conclusion to his sentence, Toni finally rushed over to intervene, no doubt having sensed the steam valve on Hovelan's impending water-heater explosion of rudeness.

"Thank you *so* much for coming down to our taping," she said, smiling down at the woman while patting her reassuringly on the back. "It's so generous of you to share this beautiful piece with us." She gave the woman's forearm a practiced upward tug, which brought her to her feet.

"If you'll look right over there," Toni said, grasping the woman's shoulders and gently aiming her body toward a long table near the convention hall's exit, "we have refreshments for our departing guests. Please help yourself—those little chocolate doughnuts are *so* good." Toni then scooped up the Declaration of Independence print and handed it to the woman before giving her a polite little shove. The woman marched forward on command, leaving the appraisal area, seemingly in a daze as to what had happened. It was a beautiful maneuver—one Hovelan had seen Toni use on many occasions. She was full of remarkable little skills like that.

Toni gave Hovelan a reproachful look but didn't say anything immediately. She didn't have to; he knew sinking his teeth into potential pledge-drive donors was frowned upon, but sometimes it couldn't be helped. It would be one thing if the ignorant only occasionally turned up during tapings of the *Roadshow*, but they were hardly the exception to the rule.

For every item actually featured on *Antiques Roadshow,* the appraisers had to evaluate over a hundred other items not interesting enough to merit camera time. Nearly half of these could be charitably classified as garbage. This didn't stop their owners from bringing them in, though. They came in by the battalion, brandishing their broken Bakelite *Mr. Peanut* lamps, their boxes of yellowed newspapers, their woefully bent *My Favorite Martian* toy antennae, their tattered old comic books, flaking *National Geographics,* and other yard sale ephemera. They brought it all proudly, along with their dreams of untold riches and perhaps an autograph from the *Roadshow*'s host. Such was the price, Hovelan had long ago decided, of doing a television show about antiques in a country where a century was actually considered a long period of time. He would love to be an appraiser on the original BBC version of *Antiques Roadshow*, where his skills could be put to better use. If nothing else, in Europe there would be far less chance of yokels turning up with Declaration of Independence reprints found in a painting in their grandmother's attic. It seemed like he saw one in every city on the *Roadshow* tour, regardless of its proximity to any of the original colonies. Here in coastal Virginia, of course, it was to be expected—not that this particular city was in any way colonial, despite being only a short drive from Williamsburg.

Hovelan glowered in the direction of the first of the generalist tables, where the appraisers and producers whose job it was to weed out the quarter-bin crowd were stationed. He had long suspected them of intentionally letting people bearing Declaration of Independence prints through to his table just to irritate him. If he didn't know such a thing was quite impossible, Hovelan would swear someone had been going around for decades putting worthless prints of the document into the backs of attic paintings just to irritate him as well.

Toni cleared her throat, bringing Hovelan's attention back to the present. She was standing over him wearing her red, all-business, ladies' suit with the short skirt that showed off her shapely caramel-brown legs. Hovelan noticed that her lipstick matched the redness of her suit. He also noticed that those red lips were currently curved into an odd predatory sort of smile.

"I'm sorry if I got a little carried away with that one," he said.

"Oh, don't you worry about that at all, Phil," she said. "Being an ass is hardly a crime. I sometimes think we'd have a lot fewer appraisers if it was." Toni laughed, but kept an eyebrow raised as well, as if daring him to argue. Hovelan tried to chuckle along good-naturedly, but there was something about her manner that was putting him off his ease. It was as if she was cherishing some warm inner thought involving him. Her laughter was not nice laughter. It was *You don't see the sandbag plummeting toward your head* kind of laughter.

"I take it you haven't seen her, yet?" Toni asked.

"Seen whom?"

Toni's predatory smile widened. "Her," she said, pointing one of her shiny red nails across the mass of antiquities and their owners, lined up like cattle along the convention hall floor. He wasn't sure who he was supposed to be looking for, but he knew it couldn't be good if Toni was so happy about it. Then his eye caught a flash of silver and his mouth dropped open of its own accord.

"It can't be…"

"Oh, yes, it can," Toni said.

"I don't believe it. I thought for sure she must have kicked off by now."

"No, no," Toni said with her widest grin yet. "Miss Zeddie is here, in the flesh, and as feisty as ever."

Hovelan stared at the old woman seated at the clocks and watches table, some fifty feet away, across the blue banner-strewn convention hall floor. He was amazed he had overlooked her until now, since her table was practically parallel with his own. Even with her back turned to him, though, he knew it was her. He would have known even without her trademark pinned bun of white hair or the gnarled, silver-gripped cane leaning against the table beside her chair.

"What in the hell is that wrinkled sack of bones doing here again?" he snarled.

"From the looks of it," Toni said, "she's appraising."

"I thought she was never coming back again. That-that-that," his voice stammered without his bidding, "she was too old to travel, or something."

"Oh, Miss Zeddie didn't have to travel," Toni said. "This is her home town." She peered back across the floor to where the silver-haired lady was seated at her appraisal table, speaking to a guest and one of the other producers. "She looks just as energetic and spry as ever, to me. Wouldn't you say so?"

Hovelan glared at her. "You did this on purpose, didn't you?"

"I wish I could say I did, Phil. I really, really do," Toni said. "I'm afraid this was all Miss Zeddie's doing. She gave us a call when she heard the tour was coming to the area. We always invite local guest-appraisers, so it just made sense to invite one of our former regulars back, too. And check this…" Toni poked Hovelan in the arm with the point of a fingernail. "She's already lined up three on-camera segments for us and is working on a fourth."

"How very nice for you," Hovelan said.

"Mmm hmm. Gonna be a busy day with Miss Zeddie around," Toni said. "You ready for your next item, Phil? I think I saw a painting or two in the line I could bring over." She allowed a pause. "If you like, I could send Miss Zeddie by to help you with them?" She flashed him the predatory smile again.

"Absolutely not," he said, practically spitting. "You keep her away from me!"

"I can't promise that, Phil," she said. "After all, I'm not her producer any more, am I?" Toni's face seemed deadly serious for a few seconds, before breaking into the grin. "Got a fun day ahead of us, don't we?" She turned on her red-leather heel and departed, her *sandbag on its way* laughter cutting through even the noise-level of the convention hall floor.

It had been over two years since Hovelan had last set eyes on Miss Zeddie and four years since he first met her. The old woman had traveled with the *Roadshow* for at least two seasons before he joined the appraisal staff, though he had never received a definitive answer on this from any of the crew. Even after he came on board, their paths had not crossed until midway through his first tour.

As a gallery owner, it was beneficial for Hovelan to be a generalist when it came to appraising antiques—as opposed to many of his non-affiliated colleagues who often were more specialized in their expertise. This being the case, many of the more interesting items that were brought to the *Roadshow* tended to pass directly to the specialists' tables. In his first season, it took five shows before anything the producers deemed camera-worthy came his way—an exquisite oil painting by a minor 18th century Italian master named Glens Richardi.

As the tape rolled, Hovelan had expounded upon the painting and its creator. He actually knew quite a bit about Richardi, whose works were among a handful stolen from the Louvre, back in the '90s. The painting that day had not been one of the stolen ones, but it was nevertheless an interesting specimen called "Looking Glass Bay." Hovelan explained that Glens Richardi had been the equivalent of a rock-star back in 1767 Florence—the bad-boy painter, who drank and caroused most of his days, only seeing fit to bring brush to canvas under threat of being severed from his patron, and even then only after a week's sobriety. He was disparaged by many of his peers, but his sheer ability when in full command of his faculties had made him a force. Richardi had produced a relatively small number of masterful works before death from consumption at age 28.

Hovelan had felt in prime form during his recounting of the Richardi legend. He had even mused silently to himself that his performance would likely establish him as the *go-to* guy for engaging appraisals among the *Roadshow* staff. Flourishing his hand in the painting's direction, Hovelan had been about to announce its appraisal value in the $30,000 to $50,000 range when a voice from off-camera piped in saying, "It's a fake."

Both Hovelan and the camera had whipped around to see who would dare make such a proclamation, only to find it was none other than the little old lady from the clocks and watches table, Miss Zeddie.

At first, Hovelan hadn't even known how to react. No one had ever questioned one of his appraisals before. However, as it had been one of his fellow appraisers making the claim and as the whole thing was being recorded, Hovelan opted for the polite route.

"Why do you think so?" he had asked in as genial yet-still-skeptical a fashion as he could manage.

Miss Zeddie had then walked past Hovelan, as if he were somehow insignificant to the issue at hand, and proceeded to explain, for the camera, that this "Looking Glass Bay" was actually a skilled reproduction by the infamous 20th century forger Elmyr de Hory. The cameras had focused entirely on Miss Zeddie as she went on to describe how the painting was an example of de Hory's later work, when his forgery skills were not as sharp as they had once been. And while some of de Hory's works were worth considerable sums as examples of the craft of a master forger, the minor flaws in this particular example made the painting far less valuable. During her lecture, Hovelan was shoved aside—literally shoved by producers and crew alike—in order to showcase Miss Zeddie. And when the segment aired, months later, Hovelan's part had been completely edited out. From that day forward, the senior producers gave standing orders that all paintings were to pass by Miss Zeddie's table to be declared genuine before moving on for appraisal by others—others which, for the remainder of that season, had not included C. Phillips Hovelan. It was utterly insulting.

If this were the only incident, Hovelan could have seen fit to forgive and forget. However, as that season's tour progressed, Miss Zeddie had become an even more aggressive thorn in his side, always appearing when he least wanted her around, tossing out unsolicited commentary about items on his table. Through it all, she never seemed to pay him any mind whatsoever, to the point of seeming not to recognize him when he confronted her directly.

Despite his many complaints, the producers of the show had allowed her to continue and often became eager accomplices in her appraisal coups. After all, Miss Zeddie always made for a colorful and informative segment, and they proved more than willing to edit out anyone who got in her way.

"She does it to all of us, once in a while," a fellow appraiser, Clifford Steigs, had said upon hearing one of Hovelan's laments on the subject. "You've got to realize, Zeddie's probably forgotten more about antiques than any of us will ever know. She's brilliant at it. You could almost swear she knows each piece she appraises on some kind of personal level."

"I don't care," Hovelan had countered. "It's unprofessional how she undermines me at every turn. How can anyone justify the… the rudeness of it?"

"Easy," Steigs said. "She's always right."

This, Hovelan decided, was the crux of it. The old bag wasn't acting this way to try and help her juniors become better appraisers; she was showing off to make everyone else look bad.

Hovelan was so infuriated that he had decided to leave the show after the conclusion of the tour. That is, until one of his rare uninterrupted on-camera segments resulted in a swell in his gallery's business. This helped to soothe his bruised ego. His business partners also insisted that he return for the next season, so Hovelan decided that perhaps Miss Zeddie wasn't so bad after all. It was a decision he would live to regret.

By the end of his second season the only thing required to send Hovelan into a fit of snarling rage was the approaching tap of the old woman's walking stick. Miss Zeddie's behavior had been worse than ever, and no amount of ire vented toward her seemed to have any effect. It was again as though she regarded Hovelan as being beneath her notice, an attitude which enraged him all the more.

Hovelan had found himself in the possession of a burning need to provoke a reaction from her—to somehow force her to pay attention to him—and he began to make plans.

On the last day of taping, in their final city of the second season, Hovelan had chosen an appraisal table within sight of Miss Zeddie's station, where he could keep watch on her throughout the day and wait for his moment. For all his watchfulness, Hovelan nearly missed it. In the midst of appraising a *Syroco Wood* corkscrew in the shape of Senator Volstead, architect of Prohibition, his eye had been caught by the red light of Miss Zeddie's video camera, signaling her first on-camera appraisal of the day. Hovelan had immediately excused himself, then dashed across the convention hall floor to take up a position behind one of the two cameramen covering Miss Zeddie's table. Through the camera's monitor he could see the old woman inspecting a silver pocket watch in the shape of a skull. It had a matching silver chain composed of tiny linked silver bones. Attached to the end of the chain's fob was a keywind, cast in the shape of a small skeletal hand. Miss Zeddie's own thin fingers then deftly flipped the top of the skull back from just behind the jaw, revealing the clock face beneath it. And it had been at that moment that Hovelan knew exactly what he would do.

"Made in 1931, but still in working order, I see," Miss Zeddie proclaimed. "Never had any need of repairs, either?" Her question sounded almost like a statement, but the watch's owner confirmed it had never been repaired, all the same. Hovelan couldn't see her guest, for the camera itself was blocking his view and the shot on the monitor was still a close-up of the watch.

A moment later, the red light on the camera in front of him turned off and its operator had pulled the view into a wide shot of Miss Zeddie and her guest—a balding, middle-aged man wearing an unremarkable brown plaid sport coat. The camera's light came on again.

Miss Zeddie had continued, "I would say that a 1931 pocket watch of such original design and superb condition would fetch twelve hundred dollars at auction. At the very least."

Hovelan had then made his move.

Stepping into the camera's wide view, Hovelan grasped the old woman by the shoulders and said, "But would anyone care to speculate how much Miss Zeddie's old bones would fetch at auction? They're at least as old as the watch."

Everything had become very still. The faces of the cameramen had gone pale. Miss Zeddie's segment producer, Toni, had dropped her clip-board. The people standing nearby in line had even stopped jabbering to one another to give the scene a collective look of shock.

Hovelan had stood there before the cameras and lights, gazing triumphantly down at Miss Zeddie, awaiting the moment when her composure would crack and she would… Well, he didn't know what he had expected her to do. He couldn't picture her bursting into tears, but he also couldn't picture her turning around to punch him, either. Perhaps righteous indignation? Yes, that's what he could settle for—a good face full of righteous indignation.

Miss Zeddie, however, had not chosen to cooperate.

Rather than losing composure, or even making eye-contact with Hovelan, she simply turned to her guest and said, "Thank you, Mr. Adriel, for coming out and bringing us such an exquisite piece."

Hovelan was instantly furious. Once again the old woman had ignored him. She was steadfastly continuing her appraisal as though he had not been there at all, allowing the show's editors plenty of space to crop him out of the shot in post-production.

Defeated, Hovelan's gaze had wandered over the faces of those in the crowd around him, which were by then softening from shock to pity. He saw Toni's fierce glare, and felt the continuing blind refusal of acknowledgement radiating from Miss Zeddie, who was still chatting with her guest.

Hovelan had seen her guest through the camera monitor earlier. And, focused as he was on Miss Zeddie's face, he could only see her guest with his peripheral vision. Something about it, in that moment, had caught his attention, though, because it did not match up to his memory of the balding, middle-aged man in the plaid sport coat from before. For an instant, his brain registered the man's appearance as that of a handsome, fair-haired young man wearing a white suit. Only, when Hovelan had then turned to actually look at her guest full on, the man appeared to be neither a balding man in a sport coat, nor younger and fair-haired at all. Instead, seated beside Miss Zeddie, its arms folded neatly in its lap, was the angel of death.

Hovelan had never before seen the angel of death, at least not outside of medieval paintings by Hieronymous Bosch. However, there had been no mistaking the identity of the terrible visage of gloom and decay seated there before the camera. Its partially exposed skull had gleamed brightly beneath the studio lights. It was a sight that had pressed apocalyptic buttons in the racial memory centers of Hovelan's brain.

A small, clinched gasp was all that had escaped from Hovelan's throat. He staggered backward for a moment. Then the floor had seemed to lurch from beneath him, much as his world had been turned upside down moments before. Before Hovelan's consciousness had slipped away from him completely, he heard the cold, distant voice of the angel of death. "You're quite welcome," the angel of death had said. "It's one of my favorites."

Hovelan had awakened some time later to find Toni shaking him and calling his name.

"I don't think he's breathing," Toni had said, looking him dead in the eyes. She then slapped him hard across the face. "Nope, looks like I was wrong," she added.

His head was throbbing with pain on the side that had struck the floor, and then from Toni's slap, but Hovelan still had enough wits about him to remember what had put him down. The man in the plaid sport coat had gone, though.

Soon enough, the executive and senior producers had appeared. They had not asked if he had been injured by his fall. No one had offered to help him up from the floor. No one said a word about any angels, of death or otherwise, having been spotted at the appraisal table. Instead, everyone had been terribly concerned with Miss Zeddie's well-being.

A meeting of all involved parties was convened in one of the conference rooms of the convention center. Video of the entire incident had then been reviewed. It played out exactly as it had occurred, from the start of the appraisal through Hovelan's interruption and subsequent fainting spell. This time, however, the balding, middle-aged man in the unremarkable brown plaid sport coat remained a balding, middle-aged man in an unremarkable brown plaid sport coat throughout. It had then been the consensus of the various producers and muckity mucks that C. Phillips Hovelan's behavior had not been of the kind any of them wished to see in appraisers associated with the show. The consequences of this consensus were left, for the moment, unspoken.

Hovelan had no reply in his own defense. His head had been clouded in a fog of pain and uncertainty and he felt he could do little more than bear their anger. Among those at the meeting, however, there had been one dissenting voice.

"Why is everyone so upset over this?" Miss Zeddie had asked, traces of an actual smile poking at her lips. "It was only a joke. I thought it was very funny. Particularly when Mr. Hovelan fainted." The old woman had then moved over to Hovelan, concern practically dripping from her face. She had patted him on the arm and said, "Are you sure you're feeling all right, Mr. Hovelan? Is there anything you need?" This, he later decided, had been the most bewildering part of the entire day. Her seemingly friendly acknowledgement made his knees feel wobbly again. As if sensing it, the old woman had said, "You just have a seat, now, Mr. Hovelan. You're in no condition to stand."

Hovelan felt dizzy again, but allowed the old woman to guide him to one of the conference table's chairs.

"Toni," Miss Zeddie added, "Would you please get Mr. Hovelan an ice pack for his poor head? That's a dear... There's an angel."

And she had said this last part while looking directly at him.

She said angel.

Just like that, she said the word.

Did she know?

Had she seen it, too?

Hovelan's memories of what had happened immediately after that were fuzzy. The producers were still angry, but they didn't seem able to get much traction out of it in the face of Miss Zeddie's kind acceptance. Her words had been few, but they seemed to disarm the situation entirely. There was no more talk of firing anyone nor of disciplinary action of any kind. The meeting would probably have ended of its own accord, even if a local volunteer worker had not run in at that moment to tell them that someone had died of a heart attack in one of the lines downstairs. The room was cleared, save for Miss Zeddie and Hovelan, who stared at each other across the conference table.

"Look," Hovelan had started, after what seemed like minutes had passed in silence, "if you somehow think I'm going to apologize…" He stopped. His pride was hurt, but his hold on reality felt even more bruised. "Did you see it?" he had asked. "Did you really see it, too?"

The old woman sniffed. “I don’t like you, Mr. Hovelan. You are arrogant and you are a sloppy appraiser. One day, it will be the end of you.”

“I think today it almost was.”

“No,” she said, standing up and gathering her cane. “No, it wasn’t.”

Hovelan had fully expected not to be invited back for the following year’s tour, and this was fine by him. He had thrown himself into his work at the gallery and tried gamely to forget what had happened. When thoughts of it bubbled up, he told himself that anything odd he might remember having seen was probably dreamed up during his state of unconsciousness, no doubt brought on by nerves and agitation and possibly a concussion.

In early spring, however, he received a letter of invitation to join the upcoming tour and for reasons unknown to him, he had said yes.

On his first day back, he learned that Miss Zeddie had not returned. Her producer, Toni, was now his producer, having been demoted from clocks and watches to riding herd over the generalists. No one seemed to know why Miss Zeddie had not chosen to return, though everyone seemed to have a theory. Hovelan, perhaps gleefully, held the belief that he was somehow responsible, but he kept this to himself.

Now she was back.

Over the course of the rest of the morning, Hovelan saw over twenty-four items pass his table, none of them worthy of camera-time. He didn't bother to tell their owners why, he just examined their items and had Toni shuffle them aside to make way for more refuse-bearing yokels with fortune and glory in their hearts. Miss Zeddie, on the other hand, had seen two items which were evidently camera-worthy by the amount of red lights he could see in her direction. By the time a second person pulling a Radio Flyer wagon filled with torn and dog-eared stacks of *National Geographic*, he knew something was up. There had been one too many conspiratorial winks among the generalist staff for this to be coincidental.

"I know what you're trying to do," he told Toni. "You're trying to sink me for this show."

"Why Phil, whatever do you mean?" Toni said, smiling insincerely.

Hovelan stepped closer to her and dropped his voice low. "I'm going to go have my lunch now," he said. "When I return, I expect all the chaff I've been seeing to be swept away. Or else."

"Or else what?" Toni said.

Hovelan smiled at her in what he hoped was a disconcerting manner. He didn't actually have any solid notion on how to back up his threat, but hoped Toni's imagination would do the work for him.

One half-hour later, Hovelan returned to his table, took his seat and awaited the first shining, brilliant camera-quality antiquity of the day. This close to the nation's capital, he was hoping for something in the league of an original J. Edgar Hoover party dress. However, there was no queue of hopefuls leading to his table as there had been before lunch. There was no line even near his table. Either Toni had dispatched them to other appraisal stations or she had abandoned him to solitude entirely. His threat had apparently not worked.

Hovelan was just beginning to calculate the level of the angry tantrum he would throw before leaving the building, when he spied Toni approaching.

"Oh, Phil. Good! You're back," Toni said. She seemed genuinely pleased. "We've got a guy in line who… well, he has something a little unusual. I thought you might want to take a look."

"What is it?" he said cautiously. Despite her demeanor, this was probably still a trick.

"That's just it," she said. "I'm not exactly sure how to classify it. It's the kind of thing that would usually go to the silver table, except it isn't silver. Or maybe tools and implements…"

"What *is* it?"

"It's a—" she said, then stopped. "No, you really have to see it for yourself. I may only have been in this business for a few years, but something about this thing tells me it's special. Frankly, I was going to send it to Miss Zeddie, but she's got herself booked solid for the rest of the day."

"And, of course, you're no longer her producer," Hovelan said.

Toni cut her eyelids to half-mast. "You don't want to see it? Fine. I'll send you something else. There's a guy in line with an ash tray he thinks was once the ear of that big robot from *The Day the Earth Stood Still.*"

"No, no. I'll take the mystery object. Thank you," Hovelan said.

When Toni returned, a minute later, she brought with her the most peculiar person he had ever seen.

The man was thin, no taller than Toni herself, with short black hair, pale skin, and circles under his eyes, as though he hadn't slept in days. He wore khaki pants, a white button-up shirt and a long taupe-colored over-coat. There was something about this man, though, that struck Hovelan as somehow out of place. It was a similar effect to how people in early, turn-of-the-century photographs never look as though they would fit into modern times; almost as if they were of a style of human being that had gone out of fashion. This particular man's style of human being, however, suggested that he would have been completely out of place in a photograph from any decade. Hovelan couldn't quite put his finger on what it was that caused this effect. It wasn't his clothing, per se, for it looked new enough to have been purchased off the rack from a local *J.C. Penney*. Perhaps it was how his clothes hung on his body, in a way that suggested they didn't belong there, either. *A tunic,* Hovelan thought. *This man would look right at home in a tunic.*

Toni turned to the man. "Mr. Furcifer, this is C. Phillips Hovelan, one of our generalist appraisers. He'll be happy to examine your... object."

"Thank you," the man said in a low voice. Toni stepped a polite distance away from the table, but remained within ear-shot.

Hovelan continued to stare at the man for several seconds before finally coming to his senses and offering him a seat. Furcifer sat down, somewhat nervously. He remained still for a few moments, then glanced into the crowd lined up on one side of the table, searching.

"How can I help you?" Hovelan said after nearly half a minute had passed. Only then did the man look back at him before reaching into the interior of his coat. He withdrew an object which he then placed onto the green, felt, surface of the table.

It was a fork—a small, two-tined, wooden fork, which appeared as though it might have been carved as a single piece from a forked branch of a tree.

As a work of craftsmanship, it was entirely unremarkable, for there was no design to it at all. One could easily have mistaken it for a failed whittling effort or even an accident. However, there something about this fork which, very similar to Furcifer himself, made the hairs stand up on the back of Hovelan's hands and neck. Something told him that in all the world, there was no other fork quite like this one. There was a primal quality to it—a force very old and very powerful, which seemed to vibrate from it in waves, spreading through the surface of the table and into Hovelan's bones.

"Where…" Hovelan began, but his voice failed him momentarily. He swallowed hard and tried to look away from the fork itself. He poured himself a cup of water from the pitcher nearby, sipped and tried again.

"Where did you find this piece?"

Furcifer's brown, almost black eyes looked at him distantly.

"It was carved, long ago, from a beech branch, near the river." There was a trace of an accent in his voice, but Hovelan couldn't place it. He didn't ponder it for long, either, as his attention was pulled back to the fork itself. The strange waves from it felt as if they were playing across his brain. He seemed to recall having felt this sensation, or something similar to it, in the past, but couldn't fully focus on any one memory.

"You may hold it, if you like," Furcifer said. He slid it across the felt until it was equidistant from both men, then he released it.

For a long time, Hovelan simply stared at it. It pulled at him like gravity. Something in his head told him he shouldn't touch it, but he found his hand reaching for it all the same. The moment before his fingers were about to close around its handle, though, there came a familiar tapping sound from the floor nearby.

"What's the matter, Mr. Hovelan? Never tried to appraise an archetype before?"

Hovelan looked up to see Miss Zeddie standing in the aisle, regarding him grimly. Anger tickled at him from a distance. "Um… What?" he said.

"An archetype," she said. "They can be tricky to handle. You should use tongs."

The gravity of the fork seemed to weaken as Hovelan's anger became suddenly less distant. He could scarcely believe the old woman had dared set foot in his presence, let alone interrupted him to meddle in one of his appraisals yet again. One of his eyebrows began to twitch. All of his former resentment toward her flamed into life and he found he had the overwhelming urge to scream at her. Instead, someone else did.

"You are not welcome here, Omega!" Furcifer hissed. "My business is with Mr. Hovelan. This is none of your concern." He picked up his fork again and held it close to his chest. He looked angry too, but it was anger that had to crawl through the fear on his face to get out.

"My concern," she said. "You should tend to your own concerns. Such as the men waiting for you outside."

Furcifer became agitated. He stood up from his seat, his eyes darting toward the nearest exit. For an instant, Hovelan thought the man was going to bolt for it, but he didn't.

"Don't worry. I won't interfere," Miss Zeddie said. "Mr. Hovelan can have this appraisal if he truly desires. I think, however, he should know the price beforehand."

Hovelan gave off a sharp laugh. "Price? I'm the one who sets the price. Or have you forgotten how it's done?"

"It's a high price, Mr. Hovelan," the old woman said without looking at him. "Higher than I imagine you'll want to pay, though I could be mistaken." She nodded to Furcifer. "You're quickly running out of moves. And time."

Furcifer's eyes flared at her hotly, but he sat down at the table all the same. He again placed his fork in the center of the table's green felt and released it. Its gravity returned and Hovelan's head began to swim again. He wanted nothing more than to run his fingers over the worn surface of this carving. Then, almost at the edge of consciousness, he found himself thinking of the last words Miss Zeddie had said to him two years ago: *"I don't like you, Mr. Hovelan. You are arrogant and you are a sloppy appraiser. One day, it will be the end of you."* It was this that gave him the strength to pull his attention away from the fork in order to glare at the old woman, who had dared to interrupt his work yet again.

As he looked in her direction, though, something in the crowd beyond her caught his eye. It took his brain seconds to register that he had seen something important, though he still wasn't conscious of what it was that he had seen. His eyes searched the convention floor, among the lines of people and their heirlooms. *Where was it? What was it?*

"My appraisal, sir?" Furcifer said insistently. Hovelan barely heard him. His brain was feeling suddenly flush with a mixture of anger, confusion and fear, each vying for dominance. Then, as if from far away, he felt his hand close around the set of cold metal tongs on the tool cloth nearby and move toward the fork.

“That’s a good boy,” Miss Zeddie said. “Always use proper care when handling dangerous materials. You wouldn’t want to become an antiquity yourself before you’ve even been given the choice.”

The old woman’s patronizing voice pierced the haze of his brain. He seized the fork between his tongs, nearly pinching one of Furcifer’s fingers in the process. As he lifted it from the table he saw the man’s face break into relief. And beyond Furcifer, protruding from beyond the edge of one of the tall, blue, *Antiques Roadshow* tapestries was the important object he had glimpsed before. It was the sleeve of a brown, plaid sport coat.

Fear seized Hovelan as apocalyptic buttons were once again pressed within his head, their force far outweighing the gravity of the fork within his tongs.

“Just—” Hovelan said, croaking from near empty lungs. He tried taking a breath, but it only seemed to come in odd-sized gasps. He could still see the sleeve. It wasn’t moving much, though perhaps it only looked as if it was moving at all because the blue banner in front of it was swaying in the breeze of an air-conditioning vent. At any moment, though, the sleeve might come into full view, revealing the rest of the coat it was attached to, and the terrifying celestial being who wore it.

*“One day, it will be the end of you,”* Miss Zeddie’s voice said in his mind.

“I… I think… perhaps… you should take this appraisal,” Hovelan told Miss Zeddie, not taking his eyes off the coat sleeve.

"No," Furcifer said, his voice now both time-lost and whiny. "No! This is not my wish. You mustn't let her do this. This is not the way it was to happen!"

The old woman struck her walking stick against the edge of the table. Studio lights gleamed briefly from its silver grip, spraying across her face as she scowled down at the little man. When she spoke, her voice was low and hard.

"You are the one who set this in motion," she said. "You must accept the consequences."

"No!" Furcifer shouted, and he began to lunge for his fork. The lunge didn't work, though. It didn't even extend over the table itself before the man's arms seized into an almost palsied state and he dropped back into his seat.

The old woman stepped forward and reached for the tongs Hovelan still held. He half expected her to shrink back, as Furcifer had, but she had no difficulty taking them from his hand.

"Are you ready for your appraisal?" she asked Furcifer. He slumped into his chair.

Holding the tongs, Miss Zeddie walked around the table until she stood between the two of them, where the light was best. Hovelan looked away from the brown plaid sleeve only momentarily, casting his eyes again upon the fork. Its gravity had diminished considerably, under the old woman's control, and the fog began to lift from his brain. His eyes then shot back to the blue banner, but the brown-plaid sleeve was no longer there.

“Pay attention,” the old woman said. “This is how it’s done.” She turned again to the slumped owner of the fork. “You are *the Furcifer, fork-bearer, tine-maker, protector of the archetype.* The office you hold had the questionable fortune to have both envisioned and brought into existence the first fork in this planet’s history.” She held the tongs up to her eye level.

Had this statement been made under almost any other circumstances, Hovelan would have felt a professional responsibility to laugh at her. And while he could feel the space within his gut where laughter should have been welling up, that cavern was empty. The very idea that this old woman was holding the archetype of the fork was ridiculous—the kind of thing that got you put away for saying, and observed for a long time afterward. And yet, Hovelan knew in his mind that she spoke the truth. The almost hypnotic grip the fork had held on him only minutes ago told him that it was the genuine article, no matter how insane the idea might sound.

The old woman continued. “Archetypes such as this are embodiments of original creation, idea and dream. They are totems both powerful and dangerous, as much for their symbolism as what they inspire. As such, it must be guarded against harm and misuse. This is the task of the office of the Furcifer.”

The Furcifer lifted his head at this and nodded.

“Haven’t done a very good job of it, have you?” she asked.

“This is not the way it was to happen,” the Furcifer repeated, tears starting to roll down his face.

"No. It isn't the way you *intended* it to happen," she said. "You intended to pass your office to our friend Cecil, here. And you intended to do so without warning him first of what the responsibilities of it are."

Hovelan was utterly shocked by this. Not the implication that there had been more than one Furcifer, nor even that this particular Furcifer possibly meant him harm. What shocked Hovelan was that Miss Zeddie knew his first name. He had gone only by his first initial for the past twenty years. He had not fully spelled out his first name on so much as a tax form in almost as long, including the forms he filed for employment with the *Roadshow*. In fact, the last time he even recalled hearing it was from a distant cousin at an uncle's funeral, seventeen years ago.

"How did you know my name?" he asked.

"I know a great deal about you, Mr. Hovelan," the old woman said, still not meeting his eye. "I've seen your role in this from the day we first met. I've seen the choices you make and the choices you don't. And I've seen what will happen to you should you choose the Furcifer's path. You would not have liked it."

"No! This man is suited to the office," the Furcifer said, sounding defensive. "The fork drew me to him. He is to become the bearer!"

"Are you in such a hurry to die that you would see your totem destroyed? With all that would entail?" the old woman hissed. "This man can no more protect the archetype from its enemies than you have. He is far from suitable."

"I am far from suitable," the little man cried.

"On that point, we can agree." Miss Zeddie turned the fork in the air, but did not set it down again. "Unlike most of your kind, you were never wise enough to hide your totem and yourself from harm's reach. How long has it been since the bearers of cup, cloth, and wheel were even seen? They remain the originators of their offices and they remain safe. You are merely a poor replacement who would have brought it to destruction."

"You are lying," the Furcifer said.

The old woman shrugged. She lowered the tongs to the table and released the fork. "By all means, then. Take your totem and leave," she said. "If I am lying, and there is no danger, you will be able to leave freely and live on to entrap another innocent someday."

The Furcifer eyed the old woman suspiciously, then stood up and cautiously reached for his fork. Once again, his hand jerked back, seized with a paralyzing fit. He gave Miss Zeddie a scornful look as he cradled his hand.

"What the hell was that?" Hovelan asked.

"Failure," she said. "The Furcifer may take no action that would bring harm to himself or his charge. If he were to leave with the fork now, the men waiting for him outside would have him for sure. It would result in harm to him and potentially the destruction of the totem." She then raised her voice slightly, projecting it in the Furcifer's direction. "If he isn't careful, his fussiness over who is to succeed him will lead to serious consequences. Perhaps for us all."

"What do you mean 'for us all'? I thought he was the only one in danger now."

Miss Zeddie frowned. "Should the Furcifer's enemies capture him or manage to destroy his charge, there is a high likelihood that life as we know it will end."

Hovelan stared at her blankly.

"You're kidding, right?"

The old woman shook her head.

"You're telling me the world will come to an end because somebody breaks a fork?"

"No. The world will remain, but in what condition would be difficult to speculate. A great percentage of its people would survive, largely unchanged. I fear, though, that this country and many others in the West would cease to exist beyond legend."

"But it's only a fork!"

"It *is* a fork, Mr. Hovelan, but it is not *only* a fork. Despite its appearance, this totem represents far more than the archetype of forks." The old woman used her tongs to lift the fork from the table again. "What do you know of the history of the fork as a tool, Mr. Hovelan?" she asked.

"Well, it..." Hovelan began. He paused as he realized he didn't know the answer exactly. The very concept of the fork seemed such a simple and obvious one that it was easy to believe its origins lost to the sands of time. "I suppose I know very little, other than its having been used for thousands of years, if not more."

"Ancient indeed," the old woman said. "The creation of the fork predates all the civilizations of this age. And yet it has only come into common acceptance in Western Society within the last four centuries. Before that, it was considered by some in power to be a blasphemous instrument that dared to improve upon the natural tool God himself had given us in the human hand." She cast a disdainful look at the Furcifer. "Such was the lot of his office as well—to be suspected and feared and often imprisoned. In fact, it was within the walls of a prison that the current Furcifer first met and was entrapped by his predecessor."

"Okay. You say they're both really old," Hovelan said. "How would destroying it affect anything?"

The old woman stared at Hovelan as if he were a child. "Mr. Hovelan, have you ever heard of a *sovol*?"

"No," Hovelan replied, irritated that she was answering his question with a question.

"Few have. I would wager even the Furcifer has no knowledge of them."

The Furcifer did not look up at this, but remained silent, staring longingly at his fork on the green felt table in front of him.

"The word sovol appears in two texts, dating to around 10,000 B.C. The texts do not reveal precisely what a sovol was, nor what it was used for. However, the context in which it is referred to suggests that sovols were as common in their time as forks today. Imagine a tool so ingrained into a culture that it is taken for granted. Imagine further how that tool becomes forever associated with the culture that produced it. And how much damage could be done by the destruction of an idea at the heart of that culture?"

Hovelan still hadn't committed to believing this line of reasoning, but he thought he could see where she was going with it. "You're saying the archetype of the sovol was destroyed, and this erased all knowledge of it?"

"Not all knowledge," the old woman said. "However, it does appear to have taken a continent with it in its passing."

"A continent…" Hovelan began, but his mind had already done the calculation. He could scarcely believe the words that were about to leave his lips, but then Hovelan could scarcely believe most of the events of this day. "Atlantis?" he said.

The legendary island-continent of Atlantis was the Holy Grail for explorers of the unknown—well, next to the actual Holy Grail, of course. It annoyed him that she'd been able to work it into the mix of impossibilities thus far

"Atlantis, Hy Brasil, Lyonesse… all names for the same place," she said. "The sovol had become a symbol of the land and when its archetype passed, so did the society that depended so much upon it. Its passing set humanity back centuries in terms of history, science, philosophy, architecture, myth and the arts. It was not the first archetype to be destroyed, but it has had the most impact on humanity. At least, until today."

Again, she brought the fork to eye level. It was such a simple-looking thing that the awe Hovelan saw in the old woman's lined face seemed almost misplaced.

"It's a strange and dangerous world out there, wouldn't you agree, Mr. Hovelan? There are a lot of deep grudges against Western culture—perhaps some with better reason than others. However, no reason justifies forever altering half the world. Particularly the half that I live in," she said. "The Furcifer's enemies would do precisely that."

"That is the heart of this matter, Mr. Hovelan," the Furcifer said. He had come out of his trance of despair and now stared across at Hovelan with his time-lost eyes. "What Omega isn't telling you, though, is that *she* is one of my enemies as well."

The old woman—Miss Zeddie or Omega or whatever her name truly was—appeared positively angry at this. "I am not your enemy, Furcifer. They are waiting outside and will be coming inside soon enough. I'm here to help you, if you will only accept."

"She wants the fork for herself," the Furcifer said. "Omega has lived a long time for a human—longer than most. But her time will end soon and she now grasps at the immortality my office brings. She does not see the curse."

"It is only a curse to those who cannot fulfill the duties of the office," the old woman said.

"The fork does not want you."

"The fork is out of options!" Miss Zeddie snapped.

The Furcifer reached across the table for Hovelan's hand, but it was pulled back instinctively. "Please, Mr. Hovelan. You are the man I have sought. You are the man who will most ideally serve."

"He will be even more incompetent than you are," Miss Zeddie said. "You allowed yourself to be cornered here. If the fork is passed to this man, its destruction will be assured."

"No," the Furcifer said, his eyes welling up again.

"I am the only logical choice you have," Miss Zeddie said. "I protect many objects of power already. Your enemies would be foolish to try and take this one from me."

Hovelan watched as the Furcifer's lip began to twitch. He wasn't certain if it was out of anger or if the man was about to weep again. He seemed on the verge of saying something further, then didn't.

The Furcifer reached out and took the fork from Miss Zeddie's tongs. He held it almost lovingly in his palms, staring at it—perhaps in to it—for a long while. Something in the Furcifer's eyes gave Hovelan the impression that some sort of negotiation was being conducted. Then, with a wince, the Furcifer brought the twig to his chest in what looked an embrace. He then extended one hand and offered it to the woman, handle first. The old woman smiled slightly and reached out to take it.

What happened next took C. Phillips Hovelan completely by surprise.

Without knowing exactly why, without so much as a single forethought, Hovelan reached out and snatched the fork from the

Furcifer's hand before the old woman had a chance to touch it. There had been no gravity to draw him to it this time. He had taken it by his own free will. Only hours later would it occur to him that, regardless of the consequences, he had at last interrupted Miss Zeddie in a manner she could not ignore.

Hovelan found his fingers fit comfortably around the fork's smooth wooden surface—almost as if it had been carved to fit his hand. An instant later, he was overcome by a tremendous sensation unlike anything he had ever experienced. It was a mixture of unity and warmth—an electric feeling that spread along his arm, into his chest and throughout his other limbs. His vision blurred as the sensation reached into his skull and began playing along his synapses. The feeling of gravity returned, only now it was emanating from within his own body. He did not feel drawn to it, so much as centered by it.

Eventually his eyes cleared and he became aware of his surroundings again. His mind had also awakened to a whole new sensory perception.

Everything around him looked… smelled… seemed young and fresh. He could sense the true age of everything around him—people, antiques, decorations, the cameras, the building itself—as easily as if they had been labeled.

There was a pie safe at one edge of the furniture line that was 135 years-old; a 90-year-old Chippendale desk; a 221-year-old tomahawk;

and, yes, even another 126-year-old Declaration of Independence print. The fork in his hand was 1,432,377 years old. In the distance, he could see that one of the show's cameramen was 24 years old. A short line of guests contained people of ages 53, 48, 56, 39, 26 and 12. Then his eyes fell upon Miss Zeddie and he saw in an instant that she was far older than she appeared. The former Furcifer was older still, at 274. And the balding, middle-aged man in the unremarkable brown plaid sport coat who was suddenly standing among them… he was far older than even the fork.

As much as Hovelan had feared him before, the presence of the angel of death didn't seem to have any effect on him now. The apocalyptic buttons within Hovelan's head remained unpressed.

The angel of death grimly regarded the old woman before speaking.

"It would be impolite of me to say, 'I told you so,' Omega… but I did," the angel said. He then took out his skull-shaped pocket-watch, flipped it open at the jaw and looked into it. "Seems we're still on for our date."

The old woman sniffed disdainfully.

"Not if I have anything to do with it," she said. Her attention then fell upon Hovelan. From past experience, Hovelan knew not to expect an extreme reaction to what he had done—not even righteous indignation. However, the glare she gave him contained the most satisfying expression of compounded irritation, frustration, and loathing Hovelan had ever seen outside of a mirror. It was exquisite. The old woman's gaze then shifted from his face to somewhere beyond his left shoulder. She gave a slight nod. Hovelan was confused at first, until he turned around to find Toni—32 years old—standing a few feet away, holding a slim black cellphone in her red-nailed grip.

"Job's over. Sheep's in the pen. Tell the sheep dogs to go home," Toni said into the phone. She then put the phone away and gave him a wink. And in that moment, a tightness in his chest he had not realized was there diminished, and the warmth of safety came over him.

"You..." Hovelan began, turning back to the old woman as realization dawned on him. The dangers Miss Zeddie had spoken of, the enemies of the fork who had pursued the Furcifer this far, had been of her own contrivance. She had herded the man into this confrontation to begin with. She had used Hovelan himself as bait. And Toni was somehow involved in this as well. How long had they been planning this? For how many years?

Miss Zeddie did not respond. She simply turned and walked away from him toward the nearby exit, her walking stick clicking against the floor as she went.

"Mr. Hovelan?" the former Furcifer said, a grateful smile on his strange, out-of-style face. He took Hovelan's hand and shook it firmly. "Thank you. You have lifted a great weight from me. You have made the right decision."

"You're… You're welcome, I suppose," Hovelan said.

Then the former Furcifer's face became serious. "There is strength in numbers," he said. "You can trust Toothpick. And when you need them, remember '*High diddle diddle.*'"

"Come again?" Hovelan said, but the pale little man didn't reply. He only smiled.

The angel of death held up his silver skull-shaped pocket watch. "Time to go, Tomasi," he said to the former Furcifer.

The little man said, "At last."

"No, wait," Hovelan began. "What did you mean by…" But, as he said this, he also blinked and when his eyelids opened the Furcifer and the angel of death were no longer there.

For a long time, Hovelan stood rooted in place beside his appraisal table.

He was now *the Furcifer*.

He had no idea what that meant nor what he was supposed to do next.

Was there a protocol to his new office? Did he have to register somewhere? What were the rules and regulations he needed to know? Had his act of defiance been worth it?

He heard the sound of high heels stepping onto concrete.

"Zeddie must be getting rusty," Toni said. "I've never heard of her getting anything this important wrong before. Guess there's a first for everything." She laid a hand on Hovelan's shoulder. "Worked out pretty good for you, though, Phil."

"If you say so."

"Hell, yes, I say so! You got to piss off Zeddie and managed to score yourself some immortality in one fell swoop. That's a payoff, if you ask me."

Hovelan hadn't quite worked out all the details of what had just happened enough to agree, but what Toni said felt right.

"So," Toni began. "It seems I'm now fresh out of a job and you're just beginning a new one. Like Zeddie said, 'It's a strange and dangerous world out there.'" An odd half-smile crossed her red lips. "You in the market for a good bodyguard?"

# About the Author

Eric Fritzius is a freelance writer, editor, web-designer, graphic artist, playwright, teacher, and actor of stage, screen and U.S. and Canadian basic cable. A former radio professional in an earlier career, he once went by the on-air-name of Erik Winston. He is a former president of West Virginia Writers, Inc. His writing, both fiction and nonfiction, has appeared in a number of West Virginia periodicals, including *The Greenbrier Valley Quarterly, The West Virginia Daily News*, and *The Charleston Gazette.* His stories have appeared in the anthologies *Mountain Voices, Dark Tales of Terror,* and *Diner Stories: Off the Menu.*

Eric lives in Greenbrier County, W.Va., with his wife and his dogs. Visit him online at MisterHerman.com for his blog and for audio adaptations of some of the stories in this volume.

Author illustration by Boyd Carr

MISTER HERMAN'S
PUBLISHING COMPANY